Buddy's STORY

DOG'S EYE VIEW

BLAKE MORGAN

LITTLE TIGER

LONDON

Chapter One
The Best Job in the World

"Oh, Buddy, where are you?" Katie's voice sang out across the field.

From my hiding place, I watched our Human come to the door of the Training Centre and raise her hand to shade her eyes against the sunshine. Katie has been with us since we were pups, training us. We do everything she tells us because we love her – but sometimes I like to tease her too. I'd found the perfect hiding place today. There was no way she'd spot me!

"What are you doing?" said my best friend, as he trotted to my side. Banjo is a small yellow Labrador and he loves to think he knows better than any other Trainee Detection Dog. It's a good job Katie has taught me to be patient, because Banjo could definitely annoy some dogs. Fortunately, he's really great at sharing his treats.

"Shh!" I said. "I'm hiding. Can't you see?" My tail wagged as I laughed to myself.

It was strange, though – as I peeked out, I saw Katie striding over in our direction. It was almost like … she'd seen me! But there was no way that could have happened. I quickly ducked down and Katie disappeared from my sight.

"Oh, Buddy." Banjo licked my ear. "You can't hide behind a mound of grass. You're too big!"

"Yes, I can!" I said. "Look." I lowered my muzzle to the ground. "I can't see Katie."

Banjo's whole body was shaking with laughter now. "Just because you can't see her, doesn't mean *she* can't see *you*. You're the biggest Labrador in the centre!"

I glanced over my shoulder at my chocolate-coloured haunches. I was still growing and my tail waved in the air like a giant fluffy flag. Maybe Banjo had a point. I gave a yowl of disappointment as Katie called out again.

"I can see you, Buddy! Stop trying to hide." A shadow passed over me and she reached out for my collar. "Come on, silly billy. Come and join the others."

The others! Why hadn't she said so before? I leaped up from my hiding place and bounded ahead. It felt great to stretch my muscles and feel the grass tickling my tummy as I ran, the morning sun warming my fur. I could hear Banjo's paws pounding the ground behind me as he tried to keep up, but no dog ran as fast as I did.

"Catch me if you can!" I called back, my tongue lolling out of the side of my mouth as I put on an extra burst of speed. Banjo howled in protest as I streaked further ahead, barrelling into the group of other dogs.

Today was our last day at the Training Centre, the day we'd been working towards since we first came here as puppies. I couldn't decide if I felt excited to go to my new home or sad to leave our first Human. I'd go to the ends of the earth for Katie if she asked me to, but she insisted my real job was going to be helping my new owner.

"I'll always be here for you guys," she'd say, as she kissed the tops of our heads each night, while we fell asleep in our baskets. "But one day, you'll need to help a poorly child. It's what I've been training you to do."

It's funny how Humans get to decide what job a dog is given, but I guess I'm one of the lucky ones – I'm going to help a child. And as

Katie has always told us: "That's the best job in the world."

We'd spent the past six months building up to this day. Each of us had been assigned a sick child with a specific need, and trained to recognize the signs and scents around an emergency. Banjo would be going to help a little girl called Rachel, who had diabetes – that's when someone doesn't have the right amount of sugar in their blood. One of the other dogs, Jet, had been assigned to a boy who had epilepsy. And me – my kid, Noah, had anaemia, which meant he needed more iron in his blood. A boy like Noah could turn pale or start breathing with short breaths if his iron levels dropped too low. If he was playing sport he could faint, or if he was rushing around he might need to sit down. Two weeks ago I'd got to meet him, so we could train together before I went to live with him. And today he was finally coming to take me home!

"Hey, Buddy, be careful!" I'd been so busy thinking about my new friend that I'd managed to tumble into the other dogs and they'd fallen against each other, their paws scrabbling on the floor. Now, they were righting themselves and grumbling in disapproval.

"You're so clumsy, Buddy," complained Tess, a Welsh Border collie. Boy, can she be grumpy! I felt like telling her that it's not good for a Detection Dog to be in a bad mood. Humans can pick up on feelings, just as much as dogs can.

"I'm sorry, Tess," I said, as she squared her shoulders. By then, a car had driven through the wooden gates of the centre and Humans were getting out of it, their faces shining with happiness.

"Never mind," Tess whispered. "The Humans are arriving now."

Swish, swoosh, swish, swoosh. Ten tails

wagged as the Humans walked over to us. Katie took charge straight away, leading the family over to their dog.

As the morning went by, one by one, the other dogs were collected by their sets of Humans. My tail wagged faster and faster with each car that pulled up – it made me so happy to see dogs and their families setting off together. But I also wanted to howl with frustration. When would it be my turn? And what if Noah didn't like me any more?

I gazed down at my glossy chocolate fur and gave my front paws an extra lick to make my claws sparkle and shine. Come on, who was I kidding? Who wouldn't want a Detection Dog as cute as me?

Katie whistled to Banjo and I watched my pal go to join his little girl.

"Banjo's been waiting for you all morning," she said to Rachel, smiling.

It was true. He was so excited, he hadn't

even been able to eat his breakfast! Rachel threw her arms round Banjo's neck and he patiently allowed her to hide her face in his fur. We'd all been taught to stay calm, no matter how a Human touched us. But Rachel was so full of fun and life – what dog wouldn't want to be cuddled by her?

When Rachel pulled back from Banjo, I felt my nostrils flare as her scent drifted across the air. I could make out her breakfast cereal, the shampoo in her hair and – what was the other smell? – ah, yes, the tang of hormones that meant she was diabetic. Banjo would need to keep a sharp nose on the levels of sugar in her blood and give her a touch of his nose when it was time for her to take her medicine. Banjo was a good and clever dog – as I watched him trot away with his new owner, I knew he'd look after Rachel.

"Take care, Banjo!" I yowled after him and

he responded with a shake of his fur, before leaping into the back of the car. As the door slammed shut behind him, I have to admit my heart ached. *I'll miss you, pal*, I thought. Maybe one day, we'd see each other again, in a park or adventure playground!

As I looked around, I realized there was only one dog left – me! My tail stopped wagging and I couldn't stop my shoulders from slouching just a little bit. I looked up at Katie's face and she gave me a big smile as she ruffled my fur. "Don't worry, little one," she said. "Your new owner will be—"

Before she could get the rest of her words out, another car pulled into the car park and a boy got out, looking around excitedly. He was wearing a baseball cap pulled down low over his face, which made it hard to see his eyes. I always like to see a Human's eyes – a dog finds the truth there. As soon as he looked up, though, I recognized him instantly: *Noah*.

When Noah spotted me he gave a cry and ran over, pulling up short in front of me. He tore off his cap and threw it into the air, whooping with delight. Well, it was quite a shock, I can tell you! But I stayed still, just as Katie had trained me to do, and waited patiently.

"Woohoo! Here he is!" Noah cried. "I knew he'd be waiting for me."

"Noah, calm down!" His mum followed after him and placed a hand on his shoulder, patting it soothingly. "I'm sorry we're late," she said to Katie. "The traffic!"

I noticed that Noah's dad was watching him carefully, as though looking for something. I recognized the crease between his brows straight away. I'd seen it before: worry.

It's OK, I wanted to tell him. *We've trained hard. Everything is going to be fine.*

"It's good to see you again, Noah," Katie said, reaching to shake his hand. Noah pumped her hand up and down in return and she laughed.

"Wait till you see your new home, Buddy!" he said to me. I lifted a paw and pretended to high-five him. He burst out laughing and his teeth sparkled white in the sunshine.

We're going to be the best of friends, I thought in that moment. *I can feel it to the tip of my tail.* I gave a tiny, affectionate lick of his hand and he laughed and wriggled.

I could detect all sorts of smells on him: worms, the dirt of the field, the tang of sweat, and something else beneath all of that – the strange scent of something that was missing. Iron. It was difficult to know when anaemia would affect a Human – but that's what I was here for. I'd been trained to notice the signs and start barking if I thought Noah was going to fall ill. He would sit down and I could fetch someone to help him, or an adult Human might notice my barks and come to rescue the situation before Noah fell or fainted.

This was called a Very Important Job.

Noah's mum smiled down at the two of us. "Hello again, Buddy. Are you ready to start your new life with us?"

"You're new to the area, is that right?" Katie asked. "I'd never seen you around, before we started the training."

"That's right," said Noah's dad. "We moved here last month. With everything that's been going on with Noah's health, we wanted to get out of the city."

"Good idea," Katie said. "It's great around here and Noah will love his new school!" She glanced back and winked at Noah, who pulled his baseball cap down over his eyes. I think he was embarrassed that they were talking about him. I couldn't really blame him – I have to listen to Humans cooing over me all the time! The cap had a picture of a baseball bat on the front, so I could guess what his favourite game was and I felt my heart speed up with excitement. I loved balls almost as much as I loved treats!

As the grown-ups began to walk across the car park, Noah and I followed. I noticed him looking at me out of the side of his eye, almost as though he was nervous. I touched the tip of my wet nose against his calf and he laughed – this was what I did with Katie, when we were out on a walk. It was my way of checking in with my Human – and Noah was mine now. He didn't need to be shy around me!

"Thank you for everything," Noah's mum said, as we arrived beside the car. The two Humans were shaking hands as Noah and I watched.

With Katie waving goodbye, I leaped into the car after Noah. I took up most of the back seat but he didn't seem to mind. As we drove out of the Training Centre, I looked at Katie one last time. She'd helped me learn everything I knew in the world. Now, it was my turn to help Noah.

Chapter Two
Home Is Where the Dog Is

Do you know what it's like to get a whole new family? It's exciting!

The car took us on a long journey, full of smells. There was the scent of hot tarmac beneath the sun and the sugary smell of doughnuts from a stand on a street corner. After a while, the aromas turned golden like straw and we arrived in a place full of trees and fields. The car went up a drive where the gravel crunched beneath its wheels and made my tummy vibrate, though that might have been the nerves. It was hard to tell.

The car came to a stop and Noah jumped out.

"Careful, Noah!" his mum called and I saw him secretly roll his eyes. His dad passed him a dog lead. It was made of woven leather in a burnished brown colour, just like my coat.

"We bought this especially for you, Buddy," Noah said, clipping it on. "Come and see your new home." As we started to walk towards the shiny front door, there was a shout from the garden and I saw a couple of girls leaping over the spray from a sprinkler on the lawn. I recognized one of them from our training sessions as Noah's sister, Lucy.

"Hey, let's go and play with Lucy and Bea!" Noah cried, and began to run towards the girls. I loped alongside him eagerly.

But before we got very far, his mum called out again. "Noah, take it easy, please!" Our run slowed to a jog, then a walk and then we came to a stop altogether. Slowly, we turned round and Noah led me inside the house, his feet dragging over the doorstep.

"You'll be out playing soon enough, pal," his dad said, plucking the baseball cap from Noah's head and hanging it on the coat rack. "Be patient."

Noah gave a big sigh. I'd heard them talking in the car and knew that Noah was on a new medicine called 'iron liquid'. Katie used to hide medicine in our wet dog food when we were puppies, but Noah's mum didn't need to do that with him. As we walked into the kitchen, I saw him take a dark brown bottle and add a few drops of liquid to some squash. He drank it straight down in one!

"Slow down, Noah," his dad said, as he took the empty glass to the sink. "That's new medicine for you. You might need to get used to it." I wasn't too worried, though. Katie had assured me that anaemia could be mended,

17

but in the meantime – it was down to me to make sure Noah was always safe.

"Come on then, Buddy. Take a look around."

As he led me from room to room, I sensed his mood improving. I sniffed the floor and brushed my flanks up against the walls, being careful to rub my scent into my new home. *This is mine now*, I thought with excitement. I wanted every animal in the neighbourhood to understand that Buddy the Detection Dog had arrived. I was here to take care of Noah and everything was going to be all right.

When we returned to the kitchen, Noah looked down at me and gave me his first ever order: "Sit!"

Immediately, I lowered my rear end and – *ooh!* – those tiles were chilly against my bottom! But I did as I was told, like a good dog.

Noah leaned down and unclipped my lead.

Then he rubbed his hand across my fur. "Good dog! Are you thirsty?" There was a metal bowl by the back door and I padded straight over to take a deep drink of the cool water. When I finally lifted my head, my whiskers were dripping wet. Behind me, Noah shook a tin and I understood immediately. *Treats!*

I sat down again and waited while Noah placed a dog biscuit on the floor. I stared at it, my nose nearly touching the treat. I stared and waited, stared and waited, my whole body trembling with anticipation. When would Noah give me the signal? Then…

"Eat!"

I lunged on the treat and gobbled it up. Maybe I ate it a bit too fast, because I couldn't really taste anything. Chicken … or ham? It was hard to tell. I stared meaningfully at the tin, hoping for another try, but Noah put it away and my tummy growled with disappointment.

"Come on. Come and see your bed." He began to lead me up the stairs, but I wove my body past his legs and bounded ahead. I could tell which was his room because of the smell that drifted out and I dived through the door. There was a wicker basket at the base of the bed, filled with soft downy pillows. *Some lucky animal must sleep in there*, I thought. *A hamster or a rabbit, maybe*. Then I leaped straight over the basket and on to the bed, turned a circle three times and settled down.

Noah was watching from the door. As I scratched an ear with a hind paw, his face split into a grin. "Mum! Come and look at this," he said. His mum came upstairs, along with his sister, who had come in from the garden.

The two of them stood in the doorway. They stared at me and burst out laughing. Honestly, I wasn't sure what it was they found so funny.

"Oh, Buddy," Lucy gasped. "Didn't you

know? Your bed is on the floor!" She pointed and I peered over the edge of the mattress at the basket. That tiny thing? I mean, it might work for a Chihuahua, but a dog like me needed room to spread out!

I tucked my nose between my paws and showed Lucy the white crescents of my eyes. *No way. You can sleep in there if you like. I'm staying up here.*

"Buddy, do you have a stubborn streak?" their mum asked me, laughter bubbling up her throat again.

I hid my face deeper in my paws. Had she worked me out already? But at least they didn't make me get down. I mean, I *did* need to stay close to Noah. Right?

I noticed now that Noah's mum was holding something behind her back, which she brought round to show him.

"I made this so you can show Buddy your life so far."

Noah took the album from her and flipped it open. There were loads of photos inside – all of Noah!

He looked up. "Dogs don't understand photos, Mum," he explained patiently. "That's like thinking they can do maths or read books."

You'd be surprised, I thought.

"You'd be surprised," Lucy said, bouncing on to the bed beside him. I looked up at her. It was like she was reading my thoughts! Maybe dogs were telepathic…

She took the album from Noah and wriggled over to sit beside me. A scent floated off her. It was a mixture of things, including crushed rose petals from the garden, but beneath that was another smell, something deeper. It was the aroma of kindness. And something else deeper still – a sharper tang. She felt … left out? I remembered that from when Banjo had been taking all the attention

22

when we were tiny puppies.

It must have been difficult for Lucy, living with a brother who was sometimes poorly. Illness takes up a lot of attention in a family – Katie had warned us about this. I figured Lucy might need someone to show her some special attention, and there's nothing more special than a dog's jaw resting on your lap! I brought my head up and rested my soft, furry chin on her thighs as she turned the pages. Noah might be my owner, but that didn't mean I couldn't spare a few moments for Lucy too.

"Look, Buddy. Here's Noah playing in the bath as a baby." I nudged the tip of my nose under the corner of the next page and Lucy laughed in delight. "See! He's turning the pages!" She hooked a finger under the next page and we all crowded round to gaze at photos of Noah swimming in a pool.

It was strange to see Noah looking so

energetic. He hadn't always been ill, which meant he could definitely get better again.

Noah's smile faded. "That was before I got ill," he said quietly. His sister turned another page and I saw more photos of him – building a Lego statue and sitting on a slide in the back garden.

"But you're getting better now," Lucy reminded him softly.

Exactly! I thought. She kissed the top of my head, as though she was reading my thoughts again. I squirmed, as if I didn't like it, but I didn't move away. Didn't like it? I loved it! "And you have Buddy here to help you get back to normal!" She handed the album to Noah and he shoved it under his pillow.

"Thanks, Mum." He climbed off the bed to give her a hug.

"You're welcome," his mum said, and then she and Lucy left.

I spent the rest of the day sniffing around my new home, chasing balls on the lawn and following Noah around. By the time we'd had supper, I was exhausted! Fortunately, Noah was looking pretty sleepy too. He gave a big yawn and I did the same. His mum laughed.

"I think the two of you are ready for bed. Why don't you get into your pyjamas?" she said to Noah.

"All right." He pretended to look reluctant, but I could see he was secretly pleased and the two of us ran upstairs.

I started to settle down for the night. We had a big day ahead of us tomorrow. I'd heard Noah and his mum talking earlier in the day about Noah's new school. Apparently, they'd been waiting for me to arrive before Noah started. I took a big gulp. No pressure, then! Katie had told us how important school is to Humans. It's like being at a dog agility competition, only it goes on for longer –

much longer. And you don't get ribbons.

I watched Noah get into his pyjamas and then pad across the landing to the bathroom. There was the sound of water running and a smell of mint floated over to me. He was brushing his teeth! I recognized this because Katie sometimes brushed our teeth with paste and a soft toothbrush.

A light snapped off and then Noah came to get into my bed – I mean, his bed.

"Shove up, silly," he said to me, and I rolled over to one side of the mattress. Noah climbed in and we lay down side by side. Our faces were so close they were almost touching and we gazed deep into each other's eyes. I don't know what Noah saw in mine – balls, treats and blankets, maybe – but in his I saw hope and a little bit of fear. I gave his hand a small lick, as though to say, *You can tell me all about it.*

Noah reached out and stroked my ears, then he rolled over on to his back to stare at the ceiling, where someone had pressed stickers of glowing neon stars. It was comforting to see them up there.

"I'm worried, Buddy," he said in a quiet voice. "What if I don't like being at school? People might not understand about…" His words faded away, but I knew what he meant. He was talking about the anaemia.

For the first time, I felt an ache in my own heart. I could protect him from hurting himself, but when it came to finding friends – there was nothing I could do to help him with that. Well, I could be cute obviously, and people always love cute dogs, but beyond that? Noah was on his own.

I wriggled across the quilt and pressed my nose into the palm of his hand. I breathed a gust of warm air out through my nose, knowing it would tickle him. He laughed and squirmed and rolled his head over so that he could look at me again.

"I'll be fine, Buddy. Won't I?" We looked deep into each other's eyes again, and I blinked slowly. *You'll be more than fine. You'll be brilliant.*

Noah smiled and switched off the bedside lamp. The two of us were plunged into darkness, but I didn't feel alone at all. I felt loved, and I hoped Noah knew he was loved too. You're probably going to say it's impossible for a dog to love his new owner so quickly, but that's where you're wrong. We recognize good people the moment we meet them, and Noah was good to his bones. And dogs, you see, they don't just like good people. They *love* them. We're all or nothing kind of animals.

My eyelids slowly grew heavy and I heaved a deep sigh as I sank into sleep. Noah would be just fine with me by his side.

Chapter Three
A New Star Pupil

I didn't get as much sleep as I'd have liked on the first night in my new home. Noah kept tossing and turning and I realized he was still worrying, even in his sleep. I was anxious too. I kept getting up to turn in circles on the quilt until finally I flopped down, exhausted.

But the next morning, we were both up bright and early. Noah went to clean his teeth again and I had a sniff around the garden. The lawn was damp with dew and I padded across, chasing the footprints of birds and cats, wondering if they had already heard about me. Katie always said I was the fastest dog in Detection Training and maybe word had spread?

I wolfed down my breakfast – biscuits with turkey in gravy, yum! – and waited for Noah by the front door. He came out with his mum following him, smoothing down his hair. Funny how Humans always like fur to be neat and tidy, even on their own heads.

"Now, you have a good day," she said to Noah. "Don't worry about it being the middle of term. They'll all be really pleased to meet you." She leaned down to kiss him on the cheek. He rolled his eyes at me and wiped his cheek as she turned to me. I stared hard at the ground so she wouldn't see me laughing.

"Buddy, look at me." I gazed up at her from beneath my eyelashes. "Now, you take care of Noah. Remember what you have to do."

Oh, I knew all right. My Very Important

Job. I had to stick with Noah at all times. If I detected the scent that indicated his anaemia was getting the better of him, I had to make him either sit or lie down until the chance of him fainting had passed. Easy! The rest of the time, I could enjoy having lots of walks, lots of company and lots of treats. How hard could this be?

"Are you sure you don't want me to come with you?" Noah's mum asked, walking out with us.

"No, Mum!" Noah cried. Then he bit his lip. "I mean, that's kind of you, but I think it will just make it even more obvious that I'm the new boy. Besides, I'm nearly twelve and I don't need to be walked to school any more."

She smiled. "Good point. Go on, then, you two. Behave yourselves!" As if we wouldn't!

The two of us set off for school. I couldn't wait to see what it was like. As we got closer, more and more students joined us in the street.

"Is that your dog?" a girl asked Noah. She looked at my shiny new lead as though she'd really love to be holding it. I couldn't blame her – it *was* a nice lead and, you know, I'm a cute dog. Noah's face flushed with pride.

"Yes. He's called Buddy," Noah told her, and she came round to stroke me before heading through the school gates. I looked up at Noah. *I told you it would be fine!* I wanted to say. I just had to start believing this myself too.

The pavements were wide here, not like in the city, and the houses were big. And the school building was even bigger! It turned out that school is *nothing* like the Training Centre. I counted – *one, two, three …* – wow, more windows than a dog could possibly count. There were several different buildings with nameplates on the doors – Dining Hall, Assembly Hall, School Library, Craft Centre… The list went on and on!

Noah gulped. "It's a big school," he murmured, as other kids pushed past him. I gulped too – it really was! We were both the new kids and I wanted to cross my paws, hoping we'd be all right. "Right, let's do this."

We quickened our pace and I gazed up at Noah, full of admiration. *You're going to be busy here, fella.* It was too late by the time I noticed the Human walking towards us, and I barrelled straight into a set of legs.

The owner of the legs gave a shout. "Hey! Get him away from me!"

"Careful, Buddy!" Noah cried, tugging back on my lead.

The boy frowned down at me.

"I'm sorry," Noah said. "It's our first day and we're still finding our way around."

"Then you should look where you're going!" the boy growled. Wow, he sounded just like a bear woken up from hibernation.

A couple of girls came over. "What's

wrong, Jake?" One of them asked, and glanced between the boy, Noah and me. Her face split into a smile as she realized what was happening and she shook her head. "You don't need to be scared of a dog."

The other girl kneeled beside me. "What's your name, boy?" She looked at my little brass dog tag and read out loud: "Buddy. What a great name! Hi, Buddy. I'm Lily." She ruffled my fur and stood back up, smiling at Noah. "How come you get to bring a dog to school?"

But before Noah could answer, I caught the whiff of a familiar scent – sharp and high, like lemons. *Uh-oh*! I noticed that Noah's face had gone pale too. It probably didn't help that the boy, Jake, had been so angry. I began nudging my nose against his leg.

"I bring him to school because…" Noah's voice was growing weak and I knew what could happen next, if I didn't do something – he'd faint!

Noah, Noah! Sit down, quick! Katie had taught me a clever trick to make Humans sit down. I came behind him to press my nose against the back of his knee so that it buckled and – yes! – he sank down to sit on a low stone wall.

"Oh my goodness!" Lily said. She shoved her backpack into her friend's arms and came to place a hand on Noah's shoulder. "Put your head between your legs." Noah did as he was told. The girl was taking charge and I licked her hand gratefully.

She gazed down at me. "Now I understand why you're in school," she said. "I've read all about you – you're a Detection Dog, aren't you?" I hate to admit it, because we're trained not to bark at Humans, but I gave a woof of agreement. This girl was clever!

I nudged Noah's backpack. That morning his mum had shown me where the bananas and glucose tablets were kept. Even though she thought I couldn't understand, she explained that bananas contain something called 'iron' which helps with anaemia, and glucose tablets are good for energy. Of course I understood – I'm a pretty clever dog!

I kept nudging the backpack, until Lily read my signals. She unzipped the bag, pulling out a banana and unpeeling it for Noah.

She waited until he had sat back up and then handed it to him. "Eat it slowly," she said.

"Here, Lily," her friend said, passing back her bag. "I'll go and get a teacher."

"Thanks, Mattie."

Mattie ran off and Jake stared at his feet, still frowning. His face was tight and pinched. I found myself hiding behind Lily's legs. I wasn't used to people frowning at me – not unless I'd stolen their dinner or made a bad smell.

I came out and wagged my tail, hoping

to make him smile, but he just backed away from me. *Suit yourself*, I thought, returning to Lily. I wasn't sure I liked him either.

"You're our new Star Pupil," Lily said to me, patting my head.

"No, he isn't, he—" Jake started to say, but Lily wasn't listening. She'd come to kneel beside me and didn't notice how Jake's face clouded with anger, but I did. I gave a whimper.

"Don't worry," she told me. "He'll be all right, thanks to you." I was glad to see Noah sitting straighter now, his cheeks pink with colour. She was right – I had done my first good turn for my new friend.

Noah had finished eating his banana and carefully folded the skin up in a napkin. "Come here, boy," he said to me. I padded over to him and he dug his face in my fur. "Oh, Buddy, thank you," he whispered, rubbing me behind the ears. "I knew you'd be perfect. You didn't make a fuss at all!"

He sat back up and I could tell how important it was to him that I hadn't run around barking my head off – I'd just let the nearest people know what was happening. *I am well trained*, I thought proudly. Maybe Noah would slip me an extra treat at suppertime?

Mattie and a teacher appeared in the distance. Everything would be all right now – or nearly everything. I couldn't stop watching that boy, Jake, as he stomped off across the playground. He paused at a corner and turned back, staring hard at me.

Even from this distance, I could see the look in that Human's eyes. They were like shards of flint – cold and sharp. Why was he so unhappy? It was Noah's first day at school and all he'd done was make Noah feel bad about himself. What was going on in a Human's heart to make them start the day like that?

The teacher came and kneeled beside Noah.

"How are you feeling?" he asked, pressing the back of his hand against Noah's forehead.

"I'm fine now," Noah said, smiling at me.

"His dog showed me where he keeps the bananas!" Lily added breathlessly. "He's a really clever dog!"

"OK, well done, Lily and…"

"He's called—" Noah began.

"He's called Buddy!" Lily said, grabbing hold of my dog tag and showing the teacher my name etched into the brass.

The teacher smiled. "OK, well, hopefully we won't need another banana today. Let's take it easy now."

He led us all into the classroom and Noah sat at a desk at the front. I really wanted to look around – there was so much to see! – but I knew that a good dog only faced forwards and didn't wriggle or draw attention to himself.

I did sneak one look over my shoulder and spotted Lily sat in the row behind us, with her books in a neat pile on her desk. She winked at me and I turned back quickly, before the teacher noticed her paying me extra-special attention. I didn't want to get into trouble already – I'd heard the most terrible stories about detention. Doggie Detention – imagine that! I couldn't think of anything worse on my first day at school. Though I won't lie – I already liked Lily a lot. She had a *great* smell and she'd been kind to Noah.

"Now, class, we have an extra-special new pupil joining us today," the teacher announced. I sneaked a look around, wondering who this could be, and realized that everyone was staring at me. *Me? He's talking about me?*

Noah got up and led me to stand beside the teacher's desk. Thirty pupils, twenty-nine pairs of eyes gazing at me with adoration. One pair of eyes frowning at me.

Oh no. Jake. He was in the same class as Noah.

I wish I knew what I'd done wrong, other than knock into him. I was a big dog, and fast on my paws – I couldn't help it!

"… and that's why Buddy is with me," I heard Noah finish.

While Jake and I had been having a staring competition, Noah had been telling the rest of the class about my Very Important Job. I licked my whiskers, trying to hide my thrill of pride. I'll be honest, my fur had bristled with nervous energy at the start of the morning but now I was beginning to relax into my new job. Katie had *told* me I could do this!

We walked back to Noah's desk and the teacher took his place at the front of the class. "All right, everyone. Maths!" There was a groan as the pupils took out their exercise books. I guessed Humans didn't like counting as much as dogs did. (I particularly liked watching a Human count out dog treats.) But now, I sank on to the floor and rested my chin on my front paws, letting out a deep, contented sigh as I thought about chicken and peanut butter dog biscuits – yum, yum. My stomach let out a huge growl that made the whole class burst out laughing. It wasn't even lunchtime!

Chapter Four
Knock It Out of the Park, Noah!

It turned out, I really liked school. I learned all sorts of things, like which animals live in the mountains (eagles and goats), how to draw a circle (not with paws) and what 10 x 2 equals (20 dog treats!). By the time the lunch bell rang out, I was ready for anything!

As Noah packed up his books, Lily came to stand beside his desk. "Would you like me to show you where the canteen is?" she asked. "It's beef stew today, followed by apple strudel."

Beef stew is my favourite Human food in the whole wide world! Katie used to feed us leftovers sometimes. My tail began to wag so hard that the tip thwacked against the back of her calves and Lily laughed, ruffling my fur. "Your lunch will come soon," she said.

I whined and Noah gave me a reassuring look. "Don't worry," he said. "Mum's spoken to the head teacher. The dinner ladies have put aside some stew for you so it can cool down." Yippee! All the quicker for wolfing it up. *Maybe I'll get a nice spoonful of gravy too…*

Lily and Noah joined the crowd heading towards the canteen. The sun was high in the sky now and the playground was full of noise as kids ran around, calling after each other, playing games. All the commotion would scare some dogs, but not me. Katie had trained us to stay calm even when there's a lot of energy in the air. Did you know that dogs can smell excitement? Oh yes! To me, it smells like a mixture of candyfloss and tennis balls. You probably don't know what I'm talking about. I don't want to hurt your feelings, but the truth is that Humans' noses are pretty useless. You guys just don't really *get* smells!

Anyway, there was a lot of excitement in the playground. Noah walked me into the canteen. And wow, the smells in there! My mouth began to water and I had to swallow hard to keep from drooling all over the floor. I could see my metal bowl over on a shelf. But rules are rules – Humans eat first. Noah got his tray and went to sit between Lily and Mattie. As they ate, a woman in a green-and-white checked apron came and placed the bowl down beside me.

One, two, three swallows – gone! And Noah was *still* eating, the slow coach. I heard the dinner lady make approving, clucking sounds as she watched me with her arms folded. "You're a good dog," she said, taking the bowl from me. I'd licked it so clean I could see my face in it. *You won't need to wash that*, I wanted to tell her, but she'd already taken it to the sink.

I waited until Noah and Lily were ready to leave. I really wanted us to go outside, where all those children were running around. It looked so much fun! But of course, I couldn't leave Noah's side. Eventually, after they'd eaten something called apple strudel, we stepped out into the sunshine.

"What now?" Noah asked, looking around. I could sense he wanted to stretch his legs, just like me. Lily must have noticed too, because she began to swing an arm through the air and pretended to throw an invisible ball. It's a good job I realized she was only pretending or I would have been chasing after that ball, through all those legs in their school socks!

"How do you like playing rounders?" she asked.

Noah's eyes widened. "No way! That's my favourite sport after baseball!"

I'm telling you, it's like these kids were born to be best friends!

"Come on, then. There's a bunch of us who play most lunchtimes when the weather's good. It's our chance to get in some practice for the school team, but anyone can join in at lunchtime." She grabbed Noah's hand and the two of them broke into a run, past a sign that pointed towards a big green field at the back of the school. I think it said: *Playing fields* – that's what Noah read out, anyway.

At the edge of the playing field was a wooden shed and Lily dived inside, coming back out a moment later carrying a wooden bat. She tossed a ball to Noah and he caught it neatly in one hand, his other hand still holding my lead.

"Good catch!" Lily said, her voice sounding impressed. I could smell the excitement coming off the two of them.

We ran over to the edge of a square marked out in white dust and Noah kneeled beside me. I was pacing back and forth, impatient for the game to begin.

As the team ran out on to the pitch, giving each other high fives, Noah whispered in my ear. "We're going to have a game of rounders, Buddy. Promise you won't chase the ball?" I put on my best puppy-dog eyes and gazed into his face. *You're kidding me, right? I'm a dog. I live to chase balls!*

But I could see from the look on his face that he meant it. He led me over to a wooden bench and gave me a command. "Sit!" I plonked my bottom down straight away, because I'm good like that. I gave him another hopeful look and I saw a flash of guilt pass over his face. Noah came to sit beside me and rested his hand in my fur.

"Look, I know you want to play with us, but this is a game for Humans. The thing is…" His words ran out and I noticed that he was staring hard at the ground in the way Humans do when they're trying not to get upset. Honestly, I don't know why they don't just let themselves yelp and whine – it would make them feel so much better.

"When we lived in our last house," Noah went on, "the anaemia was really bad. I couldn't do much at all. But then I got the new medication and we moved here and – we got you." He rubbed his face into my fur before pulling back to gaze into my eyes. "And now, for the first time, I can actually start playing sport again. It's a big deal that Lily has invited me to join in. It means she doesn't see me as someone who's ill – she sees me as a friend! You understand, don't you?"

When he put it like that, of course I

understood. I shook out my flanks and settled down on the grass, enjoying its velvety touch beneath my tummy. *You go ahead. I'll just lie here and watch.* And honestly, as he walked off on to the field, calling out to the others, I found I didn't mind at all.

Noah broke into a run, his limbs moving fluidly, and I realized I was watching a boy do what he was born to do. He ran almost as well as a dog!

"I'll bat after you!" I heard him say to one of the other players. Confident! I knew that I was about to watch something really special. I crossed my paws over each other and rested my chin on top of them. *Knock it out of the park, Noah!* I thought.

The first to bat was a girl about Noah's age. Her arms looked strong and her eyes glinted in the sunshine as she swung the bat round and – *thwack!* – she sent the ball soaring across the blue sky.

"Good hit, Emily!" Noah called, punching the air just like he'd done the first time I met him. The girl ran her heart out, racing from one post to another. It was a fantastic start to the game! I could see how thrilled Noah looked and how he couldn't wait to bat himself.

"Go on, Noah!" called Lily from her place on the pitch. "Show us what you're made of!" Oh, he'd show them all right, I knew that for sure.

He took up the wooden bat and circled it through the air as though he was testing its weight. Then he went to stand on a corner of the pitch, which was a big white square that the caretaker had marked out on the grass. Lily was rubbing the ball on her jeans to polish the leather. Even from this distance, I could see her eyes narrowed in concentration. I found I was holding my breath as I watched.

One, two, three... She started to pull the ball

back behind her. Then she released it and it soared through the air, arcing past the sun. It was like watching a bird, except without the wings! The ball flew through the blue sky towards Noah.

I'd never watched this game before, but deep inside me, I knew what Noah had to do. Humans didn't like to chase sticks – they liked to hit balls with them! *Come on, come on*, I thought. My whole body was trembling with anticipation. *You can do it!* Noah drew the stick round in a smooth curve and – *thwack!* – he hit the ball over towards the far corner of the field. The ball soared past the figure of a boy in the far distance and he reached to catch it, but missed. As he ran after the ball, I could hear his angry shouts drifting back over the field. *Whoops!* I thought. *He's not happy.*

But I was! I couldn't help it – I leaped to all four paws and let out a barrage of celebration barks as Noah dropped the bat and began to run from post to post. As he ran past me he waved and I bounced about on the spot, excited for him. My boy was playing brilliantly!

The boy at the edge of the field finally threw the ball back towards the pitch. Other kids ran towards it but they looked like Chihuahuas chasing a squirrel – they were never going to catch that thing! Noah ran all the way round the pitch and punched the air. He'd done it! He'd scored a rounder!

Lily walked across the grass to shake him by the hand and I bounded over too. "Not bad for a first go," she said, smiling brightly. "You can really play!"

The tips of Noah's ears turned pink and I could see he was pleased. He didn't look like he was going to faint and I couldn't smell any bad scents, only happy ones.

They carried on playing until there was the

sudden sound of a bell ringing.

"That's it," said Lily, glancing over towards the school buildings. "Lunchtime's over."

The players gathered to stack up the balls and bats carefully inside the shed. I walked beside Noah as we made our way back to the classroom. Apparently, they were going to study something called geography.

Lily slapped Noah on the back. "That was a good game! You should come to our after-school sessions."

Noah's face flushed pink. "Do you think—"

"Hey, you two!" a voice rang out and my heart sank. It sounded like that boy who didn't like me. Sure enough, Jake came running up beside us.

He tapped Noah on the shoulder. "I was playing in deep field," he said, "and I was watching you. Are you sure you touched all the posts? You can't sneak inside them when you're running, you know."

Ah, I thought. *So that's who I saw at the edge of the field.*

Noah's smile faded. "Of course." I nudged the tip of my nose into his palm, trying to comfort him. Noah would never break the rules!

"Jake, stop being a sore loser," Lily told him. She leaned over to us, pretending to whisper. "Jake likes to be the best at everything."

"No, I don't!" Jake folded his arms.

Lily laughed. "He also likes to have the last word on everything."

"No, I—" Jake managed to stop himself just in time, and I noticed Noah biting his lip, trying not to laugh. Jake looked from Lily to Noah and back again, then he stopped walking and held out his hand to Noah. "All right, well done."

Noah hesitated and I wondered if he'd take Jake's hand. They hadn't got off to the best start. But then Noah slowed down and held out his own hand and they pumped up and down.

"Thank you," Noah said. My ribcage swelled with pride. Not only was Noah brilliant at rounders, he was also great at making friends.

"Come on," Lily said, linking arms with both of them. "I've told Noah to come to our practice sessions. Don't you think that's a good idea, Jake?"

I heard Jake make a sound somewhere between a grunt and a squeak. I *think* it meant yes. Noah looked back at me and winked.

Our first day at school was going great!

After the last lesson of the day, Noah texted his mum to let her know about the after-school rounders session. She agreed he could play if she was allowed to come and watch.

Now, I sat on the bench with her. Noah ran over to check in with us before he started to play. His mum laid her hands on his shoulders.

"Now, remember what we agreed," she said. "If you start to feel tired, I want you to take it easy and come off the pitch. OK?"

Noah rolled his eyes. "OK," he said, then ran out to join Lily and the others.

His mum and I watched carefully. I knew Noah wasn't the only person who'd phoned her that afternoon. The school had let her know that Noah had nearly fainted that morning. I'd also overheard Noah's mum and dad talking the night before as I'd dozed in my basket by the stairs.

"We shouldn't stop him from doing things," Noah's mum had said, as I cocked an ear. "The doctor said he can start to join in with the other children. And he has Buddy now."

"Agreed," Noah's dad had said. "We want him to have a normal life."

And now, here we were, watching Noah

have a normal life. After all, he'd managed to get through a whole school day. Why should we stop him now?

I settled beside his mum, resting my weight against her leg. Together, the two of us watched.

Noah hit three balls in total and ran three whole times round the pitch. I'm not kidding, the boy was a natural. At the end of the game, the PE teacher went over to say something to Noah and then he ran over to us, dragging Lily behind him. Both of their faces were shining bright.

"Don't tell me," his mum said. "You're on the team!"

Lily and Noah jumped around in a circle, clutching each other's arms. "Yes!" Noah cried. "I didn't even realize they needed a new teammate!"

Lily grinned. "I didn't tell you that bit!" she said excitedly.

Even Jake was smiling, as he came over to join us, walking beside the teacher.

"That's a talented athlete you have there," the teacher said to Noah's mum.

She smiled, gazing at Noah. "I know," his mum said.

I could hardly believe this was the same boy who'd nearly passed out that morning. Maybe his new medicine was working even more quickly than we'd thought.

As the sun dipped in the sky, the three of us walked home together with me trotting on my lead between them. I gave a long, juddering sigh as we turned on to our street. I hadn't wanted to admit this before, not even to myself, but I'd been a bit nervous about my new life as Noah's Detection Dog. As it turned out, our first day at school together had been close to perfect. Why had I been so worried?

Chapter Five
The Golden Invitation

"Hey, wait for me!" a voice called out, as Noah and I walked out of school one Friday afternoon. We'd been there over a month now and Noah knew the names of every kid in his class. They all knew my name too, and loved to fuss over me. Noah's mum had banned me from eating treats at school, even if kids tried to sneak them to me. Apparently I was putting on too much weight!

Now, children swarmed across the pavement, yanking off their school ties in the summer sun and diving into the newsagent's for magazines and drinks. The whole weekend stretched out ahead of us, and beyond that, the whole of the summer!

Noah turned round as Lily caught up with us. She and Noah had become the best of friends since that first game of rounders. She held out a golden envelope, which glinted in the sun.

"What is it?" Noah asked, turning it over in his hand. I wagged my tail as I watched him open the flap and ease out a card. On the front was a picture of party balloons.

"An invitation?" Noah said in surprise. He read a bit more. "To the seaside!" My tail wagged harder than ever. Has anyone ever told you that Labradors love water? Because we do!

"It's my birthday next Sunday," Lily said. "We're doing a beach trip. I'd love you to come." She glanced down at me. "And Buddy, of course."

For some reason, Noah started laughing. "Do you know how smelly Buddy gets when his fur is wet?" I stared up at him, my jaw hanging open. *Are you kidding?* Wet Labrador scents are like the best combination of soggy carpet, snails and mud. What's wrong with that?

The three of us began walking again and Lily filled us in on everything she had planned. "Mum's hired a minivan to take us to Golden Beach – do you know it?"

"Golden Beach," Noah repeated. "Is that the one with the caves?" We'd been there a couple of weekends ago with his parents. It had been the most brilliant day, as one of the other holidaymakers had dropped some takeaway food in the street and I'd wolfed it straight up before anyone could stop me. Result! But I did remember those caves – I hadn't liked the look of them. They looked like ragged open mouths, ready to steal my next snack from me.

"That's the one!" Lily said, interrupting my thoughts. We'd arrived at the top of her street and she waved as she turned towards her house.

"Wait!" Noah called after her. "What do you want as a present?"

"Surprise me!" she called back, before slamming her front door shut behind her.

Noah looked down at me. "What do you think she'd want, pal?"

Snails? But I had a feeling Lily didn't like eating snails as much as me.

"Come on. I have an idea." We ran the rest of the way home.

"Mum! Can I go to the beach with Lily next weekend?" Noah burst into the kitchen, where his mum and dad were making dinner. I sniffed the air, nostrils flaring. *Spaghetti*

Bolognese! Immediately, my mouth began watering and I sidled up, watching her wooden spoon hopefully. A dog has to be alert at all times – you never know when a Human is going to drop food.

His mum heaped steaming piles of buttery spaghetti into bowls and my stomach grumbled so loudly even the Humans could hear. Noah filled a bowl with dry dog food and put it down for me. I started eating before the bowl had even made contact with the floor and half a second later, I was licking my chops clean.

"I'm not sure, Noah." I could hear the little wobble in her voice as she glanced at his dad. "You've had to deal with so many new things, recently. Wouldn't it be better to stay home and rest?"

Come on, I thought. *If Noah can play rounders, he can definitely go to the beach. And you said you didn't want him to miss out.*

Noah and I watched as his mum and dad continued to exchange anxious looks.

"Please, Mum!" he said, scrambling on to a stool next to Lucy and picking up his cutlery. "It's Lily's birthday." Noah did puppy-dog eyes even better than I did and his dad's face broke into a grin.

"Well, then. How could we possibly say no?"

The night before Lily's birthday, Noah sat on his bedroom floor surrounded by piles of wrapping paper. He held a brand-new rounders ball in the palm of his hand.

"Have you ever tried wrapping one of these, Buddy?" he asked. "It's impossible!"

I glanced down at my paws. *I don't have thumbs*, I thought. *So, no, I have never wrapped a birthday present.* Honestly, sometimes I think Noah forgets I'm a dog!

His mum poked her head around the door. "How's it going?"

Noah let out a big sigh and dropped the ball on his bedside rug. "I can't seem to do it."

His mum came into the room and kneeled beside him. She was holding a box and tipped the ball inside it. Then she took a fresh sheet of wrapping paper and placed the box in the centre of it. She cut the paper to size and folded a corner, and another corner, and another. With each fold, she asked Noah to pass her a strip of Sellotape and after a few moments she held up the box, wrapped in brightly coloured paper with a bow on top. "Do you think she'll like it?"

"She'll love it," Noah said firmly. Lily had told Noah all about her different hobbies. She seemed to do something different every evening after school. There was choir, and karate, coding club and craft night. Noah had joked that she only did hobbies that began with the letter 'c', then she'd reminded him how to spell karate, and they'd both fallen over laughing. But despite this, Noah still wanted to give her a present to do with rounders.

"Playing rounders is how we became friends," he said softly. "It means a lot."

It *did* mean a lot. Lily had become a good friend to Noah and they seemed to understand each other perfectly. She'd definitely like her present, I was sure.

"One, two, three…" Lily's mum tapped the top of each child's head as she counted them into the minivan, everyone scrambling to find a seat. Her hand paused in the air above my chocolate fur. "Ah, and you must be Buddy. Hello, boy." She stroked me and then gave my bottom a gentle tap to encourage me into the van as Lily's dad climbed in behind the steering wheel. I didn't need asking twice and leaped up beside Noah.

There were three rows of seats in the back of the van, filled with a whole party of kids, who screeched with delight as they saw my big wet nose.

"Buddy!" cried Lily's friend, Mattie. She reached over the back of the seat, her pigtails jiggling, to ruffle my fur. "Are you going to go for a swim today?"

Yes, please! I thought. How did Mattie know? Labradors love swimming, almost as much as we love sausages.

Beside Mattie was sat another friend I recognized – Ben, with the freckles smattered across his nose. He scratched the sweet spot behind my ear, making my leg kick in circles. Everyone in the van laughed.

Suddenly, there was a movement beside me and I felt the press of another pair of legs against my side. Ben stopped rubbing and I stopped kicking, and the laughter faded away.

"Urgh, your dog smells!" My heart sank. I knew that voice. It was Jake. I should have known he'd be here. Even though we'd made loads of friends at school, Jake never seemed to quite disappear into the background. He was always there, especially when Lily was around.

"Budge up," Noah whispered to me, and I shuffled along to curl up on the floor at Noah's feet. He glanced sideways at Jake. "Happy now? Buddy can't help how he smells."

"I suppose so," Jake grunted. He was looking across at the window as Lily's dad pulled out of the street. At least he wasn't picking arguments, but he seemed in an odd mood. It was almost as though I could see the dog blanket of darkness hanging heavy on his shoulders. *Why isn't he happy?* Did his mum force him to have a bath last night?

"Who's excited to get to the beach?" Lily's

mum asked from the front of the minivan. A chorus of voices replied "ME!" excitedly and hands were thrust into the air.

In the front of the van, a smaller girl was sat beside Lily's mum. Noah saw me looking and he bent to whisper in my ear. "That's Lily's little sister, Amelia. She's two years below us."

At the sound of her name, the girl twisted round in her seat to look back at us. When she saw me her eyes lit up. I couldn't blame her – I was looking pretty good in my new collar, which had neon-yellow stripes and stars on it.

"A dog!" She took out her mobile phone and aimed the camera lens at me. "Say cheese!"

I squared my shoulders. A photo! Maybe it could go in Noah's album! I opened my jaws as wide as they would go – Humans yawn when they're tired, but dogs yawn when they're excited too.

Instantly, I heard Jake gasp in horror. "He's baring his teeth at Amelia!"

All the happiness ran out of my body. I licked my lips and settled down on the floor of the van, hiding my face behind Noah's ankles.

"Don't be silly," Noah said, pulling me back out. "He does that when he's excited. This breed of dogs doesn't bite. In fact, any well-trained dog doesn't bite."

"How do I know he's well trained?" Jake said darkly.

Lily let out a long breath. "Are you kidding? Haven't you seen how well-behaved Buddy is at school, and how he takes—"

Noah suddenly interrupted her. "How he takes everything in his stride? I'm his owner – he listens to me. Honestly, Jake. You don't need to worry." His voice was friendlier now, but I knew why he'd interrupted Lily. She was going to say I take care of Noah, but

Noah didn't like having to be protected. He preferred to think of us as just a dog and his owner, just like Katie had told us that first day we'd met.

"Hey, look!" a voice called out. "We're nearly there." I scrambled to gaze out of the window as we drove through the town. There was only one thing I was looking for. House, house, café, park, arcade … beach! I gave a yowl of excitement as I finally spotted the blue glint of the sea. I remembered the salty smell of the air and the squawk of the seagulls from when we'd come here with Noah's parents. And the seagulls were all here now too, waiting to welcome Noah and me back! The strong scent of excitement flooded the minivan as Lily's dad drove into the car park.

"Everybody out!" Lily's mum leaped from her seat and came to slide open the doors. Noah, Lily, Mattie, Ben and the others scrambled out into the sunshine and ran to jump up on to the low wall at the edge of the car park. Amelia was helping her mum and dad pull out blankets and a picnic basket from the boot of the van, and as they walked over to join us, Amelia took out her phone again. *Snap, snap, snap!* Holding the phone in one hand and a blanket under her other arm, she snapped away, taking photos of us all.

"Amelia wants to be a photo journalist," Lily explained, high-fiving her sister.

"Last one on the beach buys the ice creams!" Lily's dad cried, and we all whooped and barked with joy as we raced on to the sand, running between grassy hillocks towards the sea.

I could feel it in my dog bones – Lily's birthday outing was going to be the best day ever!

Chapter Six

Where the Wild Bears Live

Noah let me off the lead and I streaked across the beach until I reached the hard-packed ridges of wet sand by the shore. The water felt good beneath my paws and I plunged into the frothy waves, barking with delight.

One, two, three – jump! As each set of waves rushed towards the beach, I'd jump over them, my legs splashing in the water. It was the best fun a dog could have without a ball!

I looked back over my shoulder to see Noah watching me from the beach, smiling to see me so happy. *Stay close, Buddy*, I told myself. I could never leave Noah for too long – what if he started to feel poorly?

I raced back to him, just as the picnic blanket was being spread out. I shook the seawater off my fur, turning my body as hard as I could. Droplets sprayed out – much further than I intended – and Lily's friends cried out, throwing their hands up to protect themselves.

"Dog shower!" Lily shouted, warning everyone. I stopped shaking and looked round at them all in confusion. What was the big deal? Hadn't they ever needed to dry off?

I poked my nose into the wicker picnic basket and felt my mouth water. Roast chicken legs! I looked around hopefully. Someone here would sneak me one, surely.

"Are you all right, Noah?" Lily's mum asked, brushing the wet hair off his face to peer into his eyes.

I'd heard Noah's dad speaking to her on the phone last night. Noah had gone to bed, but his dad had let me out for one last turn around the garden. As I'd padded upstairs to sleep in Noah's room, his dad had made the call. "He can sometimes feel faint," Noah's dad had said, "but Buddy will take care of him." *Too right*, I thought now, nudging past Lily's mum.

Noah and I settled on the blanket. She threw herself down beside Noah and the two of them tucked into some little triangle sandwiches and a bag of grapes. Everyone was eating and chatting and Lily was in the centre of it all. As I watched from my place beside the picnic blanket, I felt so happy for her.

Then the day got even better. Lily's mum reached into the picnic basket and brought out ... a birthday cake! It had a red ribbon and white icing, matching Lily's outfit.

"Come on, everyone! Let's sing 'Happy Birthday'!" The other children gathered around and Amelia snapped away on her phone. The chorus of 'Happy Birthday' floated across the beach, and my tail wagged, drawing an angel wing in the sand. I was so happy, I opened my mouth to join in but Noah clamped his hand around my muzzle and shook his head, laughing. Honestly, I couldn't understand why no one wanted me to join in with the singing!

Lily cut the cake into slices and passed them around on paper napkins printed with unicorns. Her dad was blowing up a unicorn beach toy and Amelia was wearing a unicorn rubber ring. What was it with this family and unicorns?

After we'd eaten the cake, Lily's mum gave everyone a nod as though it was time. One by one, they reached into a backpack or beach bag and pulled out a present. Ben had bought her a set of colouring pencils for craft club and Mattie had found her a toolbox for her coding club. Someone else had bought her a charm bracelet and another friend handed over a giant book of crossword puzzles. Each gift seemed more perfect than the last and I sensed Noah shrinking back beside me. By then, I knew him well enough that he didn't even have to whisper his worries to me. *Everyone else's present is better than mine.* That's what he was thinking – I knew it.

He started to shove his backpack behind him but I scrambled over the blanket to stop him. I nudged my nose against the bag and it was Noah's turn to read my mind. *We can give her our present together.*

Slowly, he reached inside and passed his gift to me. I held it between my jaws as gently as I could and trotted over to Lily, dropping the present at her feet. It landed with a soft thud in the sand.

"Happy birthday," Noah said shyly.

"I forgot to bring a present," Jake said in a low voice from beside Noah. He bit his lip as he watched Lily inspect the gift Noah had given her.

Noah's eyes slid to the side, watching Jake's face. "We can say my present is from both of us, if you like."

Jake's eyes widened in shock. "No, I—"

Before Jake could say anything else, Noah cleared his throat and jerked a thumb in Jake's direction. "It's from both of us," he announced.

Lily's eyes sparkled with delight. "I'm so glad!" she cried, and I knew instantly she wasn't just talking about the present, but also about Jake and Noah making friends.

Lily was still trying to guess what the present was. First she shook the box, then she smelled it, then she tested the weight in her palm. "I can't guess," she said. Then she ripped off the paper, opened the box and saw…

"Oh my goodness," she said, turning the ball over and over. She looked up at Noah and Jake, her eyes gleaming. "A new rounders ball. Real leather! How did you both know? I've had this on my wish list for ages."

Noah shrugged. "I … I mean, we just guessed." His face turned beetroot-red with pride.

Lily threw her arms around his neck and then Jake's. "Thank you, oh, thank you both." She turned to the others. "Now we can have a game of beach rounders! Who wants to play?"

"YES!" Everyone leaped to their feet.

"We can practise for Activity Day," Mattie added. I'd heard about this from listening to Noah and Lily – Activity Day was a special day of sports at the end of the school year and it was happening the next day. It was going to be held in a special arena – there would even be a hot-dog stand!

But Lily's face fell. "Oh no. We didn't bring a rounders bat."

"Oh yes, we did." Her mum pulled a bat out of the bottom of the picnic basket. "Do you honestly think we'd forget? It's your favourite game!"

Lily danced on the spot. "This is the best birthday ever. Come on, everyone!"

All the children gathered on the beach and organized themselves into two teams. Amelia took a stick and dragged it through the sand to mark out a pitch, then Jake placed a small pile of pebbles at each corner in place of a post. Noah stood with the bat between his hands, shifting his weight from hip to hip. He was a natural!

"Ready!" Lily had the ball in her hand and took a run up, before releasing it through the air. Noah hit the ball in one smooth movement and dropped the bat in the sand, before running from base to base, his trainers flashing across the sand! A few weeks ago he'd been playing for the very first time with Lily, and now he seemed able to read her movements, guessing which way the ball was going to arc through the sky.

The ball landed behind a sandcastle and I chased after it, picking it up gently between my jaws to carry it back to the teams. "Well done, Buddy!" Lily called over to me. "You'll be on the team soon!"

As they carried on playing, I stood sentry beside Amelia, who was busy taking photos. Every time Noah ran past me, I'd lift my nose and search the air for his scent. Everything seemed to be all right and by the way he was throwing himself around the beach, I could tell he was happy. This meant that whenever the ball was hit a long way down the beach, I didn't mind racing after it to bring it back. It felt great to run beside the waterline, kicking up pawfuls of sand. But as I turned back for another time, carrying the ball in my mouth, I noticed that Jake and Noah had left the game to drift down towards the sea. I wanted to follow Noah but I had to get the ball back to the rest of the team.

As I trotted back to the game, my eyes didn't leave Noah and Jake. I could only guess that they wanted some time alone to test out the shape of their new friendship, now that Noah had allowed Jake to share the gift for Lily. Still, there was no way I was abandoning my charge as Detection Dog. So I dropped the ball at Lily's feet and raced back down the beach towards them.

As I arrived beside the boys, they were picking their way across the rocks near the caves. Clusters of seaweed drifted in rock pools and pointed barnacle shells clustered in groups, hurting the pads of my paws as I tried to follow. My front paw slipped into a rock pool and I let out a yowl of pain.

Noah's head whipped round. "Buddy, what are you doing?"

Jake looked back too, and I saw him roll his eyes. "Stay on the beach!" he shouted, batting a hand at me. Noah turned around to him and Jake lowered his voice – but not enough. I still heard what he said next.

"Why can't he leave us alone?" Jake grumbled. "Just the two of us. I'm your friend, not Buddy's."

I froze to the spot, waiting to see what Noah would do. Surely, he'd stand up for me? But he shoved his fists into his pockets and followed in Jake's shadow. He glanced back and pulled a face as though to say, *Sorry Buddy*.

Sorry? Not sorry enough to tell Jake what a good dog I was! The hurt pierced my heart like a thorn in my paw. I started to pad after them, but my paws slipped on the rocks and the pads of one of my feet slid into a rock pool, catching on the sharp edges of some barnacle shells.

Oweeeee! I couldn't hold back a howl and when I looked down I saw a cloud of blood billowing in the seawater. That couldn't be good! I raised my paw in front of my nose and inspected it. A fine slice scored the soft underside of my foot. A cold shiver of understanding ran down my spine: this was a dangerous place.

I glanced up at the distant figures of Jake and Noah. They were heading further towards the cliff face, where even more scattered rocks were piled up. *It's not safe. They shouldn't be going there.* But if I followed, would Noah think I was being a nuisance too?

I couldn't bear the idea that my bond with Noah might be spoiled. But then I tried to imagine what Katie would say, and I knew straight away. *No way am I letting him go out there without me. I have a Very Important Job to do. Abandon Noah? Never!* In an instant, I began clambering over the rocks again, determined to follow – even with a hurt paw.

Jake's voice drifted back to me on the warm air and my ears stood up. "There's an entrance just round here." He pointed and I followed the line of his finger towards the base of the cliff, where a small entrance to a cave sat hidden in the shadows, dark and brooding. The sun definitely didn't reach in there and I felt my flanks shiver as I imagined how damp and eerie it must be inside. How could Humans possibly want to go in there? It looked like the type of place a wild bear might live!

But the boys carried on and I was forced to follow as the rocks turned into boulders. It was getting more and more difficult for my four paws to keep their grip, the seaweed was growing in thick, slippery ropes now. A dog could break a furry leg, if he wasn't careful!

My cut paw was still bleeding, I noticed. Still, I kept following them. I glanced back and noticed that I could hardly see the game of rounders now – I definitely couldn't see the ball.

I turned back to continue following them, but – they had disappeared! *Noah? Jake? Where are you?* I felt the panic start to rise in my chest and I lifted my head to the sky, giving a long, desperate howl. I waited for a response, but … nothing.

The water lapped around the boulder I stood on and as I glanced down at the choppy waves, I began to wonder if I really did like water. But Noah was out there, without me, and there was no way I was leaving him alone with Jake. I raised my muzzle to the air and tried to catch his distinctive smell to trace him, but there was only a sharp aroma that drifted back.

I knew that smell.

I took a deep breath and plunged into the water, my legs scrolling wildly as the shock of the cold took my breath away. I craned my neck to keep my head above the water and began to swim towards the only landmark that made sense – towards the cave's mouth. The sound of frantic barking echoed off the cliff face and after a moment I realized that it was my own barks I could hear. *Noah, don't go!*

I couldn't believe he'd do this – he knew how important it was for us to stay together. I paddled on, following the strange, tangy scent that I'd detected when Noah had fainted before. It wasn't as strong this time, just a wisp snatched away on the sea breeze, but it was definitely there. A trained Detection Dog doesn't make mistakes – not about smells. I knew deep in my bones that Noah shouldn't be out in the water! And he definitely shouldn't be alone in a hidden cave with a boy who didn't much like him.

Oh, Noah, what are you doing? I charged on, my legs circling through the water faster than ever, my whole body trembling now until eventually I heaved myself up on to the rocks, panting hard. I'd managed to swallow some saltwater – yuck! – and my throat felt dry and scratchy. I stared into the dark, empty mouth of the cave and howled.

I glanced back towards the beach and gave another howl, the biggest of my life, to send a message that I hoped someone would hear. Then I turned to the cave, my heart beating wildly in my chest, as I took a deep, juddering breath.

I'm going in.

Chapter Seven
Fool's Gold

The cave was everything I expected it to be – dark, wet and scary. But I knew I had to be brave. Braver than I'd ever been in my short life. I glanced around the gloomy interior of the cave but it was hard to see anything other than the choppy waves of water reflecting the dripping stone roof. I listened hard – thank goodness for my sensitive Labrador ears – and heard the sound of a couple of voices coming from around one of the cave walls. If I could just get over there…

I dipped my nose to the water, trying to judge how deep it was. I lowered a paw to test, but before I knew what was happening, I lost my balance and my whole body went slipping and sliding into the sea!

I yowled with desperation as a cold wall of water hit my ribs and I wondered for a moment if this was it. *I'm drowning!* But as I prepared to give my last desperate bark, I realized I was standing on all four paws and the waves only came up to my chest. *Well, that was embarrassing!*

I began to walk through the rock pool, testing each slippery surface with a paw before transferring my weight. I still had to be careful – if I had an accident in here, no Human would find me. But this was about more than hurting another paw – I had to be there for Noah at all times. And in order to protect him, I had to protect myself. As I glanced out towards the ocean, I saw that the tide was coming in. The waves frothed and churned around me and I had to move quickly.

I approached a stone pillar, worn smooth by waves, and I paused to listen for voices again. It was definitely Noah and Jake talking, and when I peered round the corner, the two of them were crouched over a rock pool, sorting through stones.

What are they doing? I thought. *Looking for a snack?* I almost snorted with disgust as Noah lifted a rope of seaweed and placed it to one side. Who'd want to eat that? Noah glanced at Jake, the expression on his face uncertain. "Are you sure we're going to find some?" *What, sausages? Not likely*, I felt like telling him.

"Of course I'm sure. Dad says that fool's gold can be found all along this coastline." He lifted a rock and inspected it, running a finger down a seam. "Look!" Sure enough, something glistened beneath the reflected light of the waves. It looked yellow and glittery. "I told you. This will make the best present for Lily. Its proper name is pyrite but it looks like real gold! Let's find some more."

So they had come all the way out here to look for a present for Lily? But the two of them had already given her a rounders ball. Then I realized – maybe Jake wanted to give Lily his own present, even though he'd forgotten to buy one. It made sense, though I still wasn't sure that coming all the way out here was the best idea. I heard the waves frothing behind me in the mouth of the cave, getting closer all the time as the tide rushed in. They sounded like ghosts, whispering and hissing. No, this had not been a good idea at all!

"Yes!" Noah interrupted my thoughts, holding up a nugget of yellow rock in the air, before passing it to Jake. "Found one!"

Jake turned it over in his hand. "Great!"

He slipped the rock into the pocket of his swimming trunks and went back to searching until he gave a cry of delight and plucked up his own stone, bigger even than the one Noah had found. "Perfect! Thanks for helping, Noah." He peered out of the cave mouth. For the first time, I saw him notice the waves. "We should get going," he announced.

Thank goodness! I thought. I wasn't sure I saw the point of these chunks of yellow rock. Lily struck me as the type of girl who liked people whether or not they gave her birthday presents. Jake needed to be more sure of her friendship.

I darted my head back, before they started moving towards the cave mouth. Jake had sounded so grumpy about me following them and they'd both ordered me to wait on the beach. I'd ignored their commands! But I was too late and…

"I don't believe it! Your dog's here!"

"What?" Noah didn't sound happy at all and my flanks started to tremble. I'd never trembled around Noah before. There was a sudden splashing of water and the two of them appeared around the corner. Noah's mouth hung open in a ragged hole. "What are you doing here? I told you to stay on the beach!"

But, but, but… My fur was wet and clinging to my sides and my body was shaking so much I couldn't even concentrate on making myself look charming enough to tease him out of his bad mood. I started to touch the tip of my nose to his leg, in the hope that he'd understand. But then that smell flooded my nostrils again – keen and strong – stronger even than the salty tang of the sea.

I looked up into Noah's face and saw that his lips had turned white. *Oh, Noah! Never mind me, YOU shouldn't be out here!* I glanced back at the cave's mouth, where the water was pouring in. I could feel it beginning to tickle my belly. I nudged him more urgently, hoping to encourage him to get back to the beach quickly, before the water rose any further, but—

"Your dog STINKS!" Jake angrily kicked a foot in the waves, covering me in water and half blinding me with the salt. I shook my fur – what else was I supposed to do? – and Jake gave a bark of anger. "Get away from us. Come on, Noah!"

When I was finally able to open my eyes again, Jake was dragging Noah out of the cave. They were leaving me behind again! Noah looked back over his shoulder, gesturing at me to follow, and I tried to keep up but the pads of my paws didn't have the same grip as their Human toes. The water only reached up to their thighs but it reached up past my nose!

They started to pull ahead and I could see how Noah's body was sagging and slowing down, as he pushed against the weight of the water. Jake kept yanking his arm roughly and I could see the red rings on Noah's skin from where his friend's fingers were digging in. *Friend?* I snorted – what a joke! Noah should never have come out here with Jake.

He shook off Jake's hand and clambered up on to a slippery rock, leaning back against the cave wall as the waves crashed around his feet.

"What are you doing?" Jake asked, his mouth gaping open. "We need to get out of here!"

Noah pushed a hand roughly through his hair and closed his eyes. "I just need to rest a moment," he said. I remembered this from the rules his mum and dad had agreed with him – if Noah ever got overtired, he had to stop and rest.

"We don't have a moment!" Jake exploded. But he took a deep breath and clambered up on to the rock beside him. He rested a hand on Noah's shoulder. "Are you all right?" he asked. His voice was tight with worry and he glanced over at the rock pools. Or where the rock pools had been only minutes ago. By now, they were totally hidden by the rising water. If Noah and Jake couldn't find the right route home, their legs would be torn to shreds as they swam through the water.

There was nothing for it – I had to lead them back to the beach! I threw myself into the water, like the champion swimmer I was. I mean, I haven't actually won any medals, but Katie always told me I was worth my weight in gold. And since I'd sneaked all those snacks at Noah's school, surely that meant I was worth even more now. *Here's hoping*, I thought. I had to swim like my life depended on it. Like three lives depended on it! Because, of course, they did.

Noah and Jake watched me emerge from the cave. For once, Jake didn't throw me an evil look. I lifted my head high out of the water, out of reach of the churning waves, my nostrils flaring as I tried my hardest to detect the quickest, safest route back to the beach. Beneath the surface of the water, my legs moved in fast, furious circles. *This way, come on!* I didn't even think about my hurt paw.

"He's leading us to safety!" Jake cried. Funny how he liked me now! Noah was looking a little better and his face split into a grin.

"Good dog!" he called after me. I circled round to check they were following. I saw Noah lower himself into the water, sitting on the edge of the rock. Jake dived in from a standing position. *Crash!* Water exploded up around him and Noah jerked back. I counted under my breath – *one, two, three...* Who said dogs couldn't count? Then Jake's head emerged and he began swimming towards me. Noah slipped into the water behind him and the two of them started to follow me to safety. I turned back around, my nose pointed straight towards the beach.

The sun blazed in the sky. I could make out the distant strip of yellow sand over on the beach and figures running around – the other children were still playing rounders but the picnic blanket was empty. Where were Lily's mum and dad?

"Hold on, Buddy!" Noah's voice croaked. He was struggling! I changed direction and headed towards an outcrop of rock in the shallower water. We needed to take another rest. We couldn't make it back to the beach in one go. But Jake had pulled ahead and was halfway to the shoreline. My heart almost stopped in my chest as I realized … it was just me and Noah now.

I clambered on to the rocky shelf and a moment later, Noah climbed after me. He straightened up slowly, the water cascading off his body, his chest panting with the effort.

Another huge cloud of sourness drifted over to me, more pungent than ever, as Noah's body swayed.

Noah, no! Get down! Sit on a rock, put your head between your knees. I barked so madly that the sound echoed back to me, my words jumbled up in my own ears. It was too late – he'd never understand.

He moved in slow motion at first. But then his body gained speed as it fell like a dead weight back into the sea – *SPLASH!* My best friend in the whole world disappeared from sight.

Noah! With a huge bark of distress, I threw myself back in after him and began to doggy paddle like I'd never doggy paddled before.

Don't let me be too late, I thought desperately, as I moved through the sea, which was choppy this close to the rocks. My fur was slick with water, slowing me down. My tongue lolled out of my mouth and I had to spit out saltwater to avoid choking. Finally, I saw a shadowy figure bobbing below my paws and, peering beneath the waves, I could make out Noah's face. His eyes had drifted shut, his long eyelashes tickling his cheeks.

No, please, no. I'm coming for you! I tried to send him the message, pulsing through the water. *I'll save you!*

I only hoped Noah could hear me.

Chapter Eight
Slippery as a Fish

"Help me!" Noah managed to gasp when we finally broke the surface. He was conscious again, at least.

The tide was coming in faster than ever. I leaned my flank against a boulder rising out of the water. Maybe, if I could get Noah up on to here, he'd have a few moments to gather himself. He was floating on his back in the water, so I swam round to his side. Counting under my breath – *one, two, THREE!* – I began to use my nose to push his body over towards the rocks. *Come on, Noah!*

The shock of the movement made him cry out and he began to circle his arms through the water to help himself float. He took a huge breath but swallowed some water and started coughing and spluttering. I waited for him to gather himself and then I heaved against him again.

Catch hold of the rocks! I wanted to tell him, if only he could understand. And in that moment – he did! As we got closer to the rocks, he reached out a hand and caught hold of one, using a last burst of energy to pull himself out of the water. Slippery as a fish, Noah finally rolled on to the flat slab of rock. His chest rose and fell with shallow breaths, but other than that he wasn't moving. I leaped up after him, my fur clinging to my ribs.

I went straight into Emergency Mode – the one Katie had made us run through, over and over. I knew exactly what to do with Humans who had fainted. I nudged Noah's legs and arms so that they lay straight beside his body. Then I turned him over into the Recovery Position, by tucking my muzzle beneath his bum. Next, Noah's lower arm needed to be behind him to stop him from rolling on to his back again, so, as gently as I could, I held Noah's lower wrist between my teeth and pulled. Then I stepped back and assessed my work. Noah wouldn't roll over now, for sure, and even if he was sick, he wouldn't choke.

Voices were calling from the beach by now and, looking in that direction, I could just about make out Lily and the others waving at us frantically. Her dad was striding into the water and there was another, smaller figure following him. I thought it looked like Amelia, but the sun was in my eyes and I couldn't see properly.

I padded around to stand in front of Noah's face. It was a ghostly white. I could hardly bear to look. *Noah, wake up*. At least I could feel his breath warm on my fur, and some of the scent from earlier had faded, which meant he had to be getting better again. If only he'd wake up!

I carefully licked his cheek, then pulled back to look for a response. Nothing. *Come on, come on*. I licked his other cheek – still nothing. Then I remembered the tips of his ears, which would turn red when he was embarrassed. He was super sensitive there! I reached to lick and nibble his ears and immediately felt movement beneath my chest.

"Buddy, what are you doing?" Noah wriggled out from beneath me, coughing up water. "Urgh!" He sat up and gazed blearily around him. "Where am I?" But Noah saw the caves and his face changed. He threw his arms around my neck, rubbing his face into my fur even though it had to be *really* smelly by now. "We need to get back!" he sobbed.

Suddenly, the hugeness of what had just happened hit me like a puppy rolling into my legs. None of Katie's training had prepared me for this moment. I let myself sink into a sitting position, my whole body trembling as wet fur clung to my ribs. I gave a soft whine and licked the back of Noah's hand, wanting to comfort myself as much as him. *What just happened?*

The waves were lapping at our feet now and I glanced doubtfully over towards the beach, which seemed a long way away. Lily's dad was still making his way out to us, but the waves were strong. We had no choice but to wait.

Noah dried his tears on my fur and then I walked over to the rock's edge, pacing back and forth with anticipation. I gave a bark and Lily's dad waved a hand through the air as though to say, *I'm coming. Just stay there.* Like we had any choice! But I don't think I'd ever been so glad to see a grown-up racing towards us.

Eventually, Lily's dad reached the rock and climbed up beside us.

"What have you boys been playing at?" he said, but it was clear he didn't care about the answer – he was staring hard at Noah, who still looked pale. How were we going to get him back?

I looked Noah up and down. Those long arms – perfect for throwing rounders balls. Maybe he could hook an arm round Lily's dad and we could carry him back through the water?

Ready? I yipped. Noah nodded and then the three of us slid into the water, with Noah suspended between us, his legs kicking even if he was too weak to swim on his own. Lily's dad peered down into the water, telling us when there was a rock to avoid. After a long while, my paws felt firm sand beneath them and we were able to stride through the water, Noah staggering between us.

Lily came running over to us, making a huge splash and a fuss. "Thank goodness!" Her dad scooped Noah up in his arms and carried him the rest of the way back, walking past Jake, who had a towel wrapped around his shoulders and was shivering, but I sensed it wasn't from the cold water. The sharp tang of fear floated from his direction and filled my nostrils. I snorted it back out again – I'd had enough of that feeling for one day.

"What happened?" Lily's mum asked, as she draped a towel around Noah and drew him to her in a hug. Her face was pinched and tight as she looked between us.

We all waited for Noah to say something, but he just shook his head and muttered, "I can't remember." Then his eyes darted over to Jake, who was watching us intently.

"Come here, Jake," Lily's mum called gently.

He hesitated, then walked over, dragging his feet through the sand. "You have to tell us what happened out there. I promise, we won't blame you for anything." At the sound of the word 'blame', I saw something settle in his face. I saw panic.

He suddenly pointed at me and said words I never expected to hear from any Human. "Buddy abandoned us."

"Buddy?" Noah echoed.

"What?" Lily looked shocked and her mum's lips set in a thin line. Her dad was shaking his head.

Jake was talking more quickly now, as though he was gaining confidence in his story. "He swam out to the caves so we had to follow him, but then he just disappeared. When Noah became ill, we were stranded. Buddy came back to help in the end but..." He flashed me an angry look. "He should never have gone out there in the first place!"

His words were like shards of ice in my heart. Jake's finger trembled as he pointed again. "It's all Buddy's fault!"

Chapter Nine
A Let-Down Unicorn

"Hang on, Jake…" Lily's little sister, Amelia, stepped forwards, clutching her mobile phone, but her mum gently placed a hand on her shoulders and steered her back towards the picnic blanket.

"Now is not the time for photos," she said. "Can you help us pack up?"

"Mum, wait!" she began to protest, her little face creased in a frown.

"Not now, Amelia!" her dad said. "You heard. Can you deflate the unicorn ring, please?" Amelia put away her phone and went to let down the inflatables. I watched as the unicorn's horn slowly collapsed and I suddenly felt sorry for the creature – but not as sorry as I felt for myself.

Lily's birthday had been ruined. Noah had nearly died out there and now Jake had told every Human that it was all my fault. Misery saturated me even more than the seawater clogging up my fur. I felt so dejected that I couldn't bring myself to make eye contact with anyone and sat with my nose nearly touching the sand. *Is this what heartbreak feels like?* I wondered.

At least they were looking after Noah. Lily and her parents clustered around him as he talked.

"I'm sure there must be a good explanation," Noah said, the desperation clear in his voice. I dared to look up and found him staring at me, as though he was seeing me for the very first time. "Buddy wouldn't do that," he said in a whisper.

"Here, drink this." Lily passed Noah a carton of orange juice. He sat on the picnic blanket and drank thirstily through a straw – *slurp!* We all waited for him to finish, then Lily kneeled on the blanket beside him. "Can you remember anything at all?" she asked in a gentle voice. The kindness shimmered off her like stardust. Thank goodness Noah had a friend like her.

Noah's eyes darted nervously from face to face. I wriggled along the sand and laid my jaw in his lap. I could feel everyone's eyes boring into me and I gave a small whine. Jake was staring hard at the sand beneath his feet.

"I can't…" Noah pushed a lock of hair out of his face. "I can't really remember anything. Jake and I went down to the sea and—"

"To chase after Buddy!" Jake interrupted, his face dark. "Remember, Noah? He was in the sea when we first went out."

Noah looked down at me. "I guess," he said after a pause. "But it's like everything is jumbled up in my head." *Too right it's jumbled up*, I thought hotly. *By Jake's lies!*

Ben, Mattie and the others were gathered around, making soft reassuring noises. They all held their beach bags and backpacks. The day had been ruined – by me?

Lily's dad placed a hand on his shoulder. "Noah, I am so sorry that this has happened. We should get you back to your parents." He glanced at the others. "Come on, everyone. The party's over. Let's go home."

One by one, the kids drifted back up the beach.

Eventually, it was only me, Lily and Noah left. I didn't know whether to be happy that we were finally alone or sad to think about what was to come. I thought I'd done the right thing, helping to rescue Noah, but in the end it had just made things worse. *I did everything, just like Katie taught me*, I thought. *So why do I feel so bad?*

Lily gave a big sigh.

"I'm sorry for ruining your party," Noah told her. His voice was almost a whisper.

"You didn't ruin the party," she told him quietly. She bumped her shoulder against his. "We still got to eat cake!" Noah gave a small, brave smile.

He and Lily got to their feet and began to fold up the picnic blanket. They each held a corner and came to meet each other in the middle. Noah passed the corners to Lily and bent to retrieve the folded end. Then they folded again, moving silently, almost as though they didn't need words to understand each other. It brought a lump to my throat and, for a moment, I had to look away. I noticed something resting in the sand. It was Lily's new ball, her gift from Noah.

I took it up gently in my jaw and carried it over to Lily.

"Good dog!" she said, patting me on the head as she took the ball from my mouth. She wiped off my saliva on the back of her shorts, politely pretending that I hadn't just drooled all over it.

"He *is* a good dog," said a voice. It was Amelia, gazing down at me as she clutched her phone.

"No more photos," Lily said gently. But Amelia kept staring at me, her eyes brimming with tears. What was wrong? She opened her mouth to say something, when her mum came back down to the beach.

"What's going on?" she asked. "Come on, we need to go."

We followed her towards the car park, our heads bowed. As we clambered back into the minivan, this time I didn't care if my smelly fur left a coating of hairs across Jake's jeans.

He hastily pulled his legs up and sat cross-legged on the seat as I settled down on the floor. My tail curled around my hind legs, so that I felt as small and secure as I possibly could.

Lily's parents dropped the kids off at their houses, one by one. Goodbyes were called out and Lily waved back, thanking them, but the mood of the day had turned sour. I could detect the sadness coming off Noah – a damp smell like rotting leaves – even though the colour had come back to his cheeks. His body was better, but his heart hurt like mine.

I dreaded getting home because I knew what Lily's parents would say to Noah's. That I'd been a bad dog. But I hadn't been! Noah reached down to tickle behind my ears, but it didn't make me feel any better.

Finally, we turned into Noah's drive and I slunk out of the car, rushing past the legs of Noah's parents as they stood at the front door.

"What's wrong?" I heard Noah's mum ask, as she watched me slink upstairs. I stood on the landing and peered down to watch the Humans.

Amelia was leaning out of one of the van's windows, holding her mobile phone. "Can I show you—"

"NOT NOW, AMELIA!" her parents shouted, and she shrank back into her seat, her face small and white as she tucked the phone away in her jeans pocket.

"Can we talk?" Lily's dad said, and there was the sound of footsteps as they all went into the kitchen and closed the door. I ran into Noah's bedroom, flattening my body to crawl under his bed.

Then I waited. It was the longest wait of my entire life, longer even than waiting for supper. I licked a patch of my fur, over and over, until the skin turned red and sore. Then I rested my chin on my paws and tried to sleep, but it was no good.

Eventually, I heard footsteps on the stairs and watched two sets of legs walk into Noah's room. There was a small grunt and someone sat down on the floor beside the bed and a hand was placed gently on the carpet. Despite my better instincts, I crawled over and tentatively licked the top of the hand. Noah beckoned me out from beneath the bed. Beside him sat his mum. Both of them were looking at me. My stomach gave a small growl.

Noah's mum reached over and patted my head. "You can have supper soon." She sighed. "There's no point punishing him now. Too much time has passed. He won't realize it's to do with his behaviour on the beach."

Noah sighed too. In his other hand, he held a rounders ball and was turning it over and over. I sniffed the leather and looked at him hopefully, but Noah shook his head. His mum took the ball from him and placed it on his bedside table. She took his hand and held it between hers.

"I've spoken to Lily's parents. It sounds like that was quite a shock at the beach." She didn't look at me or Noah, just gazed into the middle distance as though she was thinking hard.

"Mum, I'm not sure it was Buddy's fault," Noah said. He was looking at me, but I could barely make eye contact with him.

His mum gave a big, shuddering sigh. "The fact is, you can't remember, Noah. And apparently Jake can." Finally her gaze switched over to me and I felt my whole body flinch. "This has clearly been too much for you. Your dad and I have been talking. No more sport."

"What?" Noah asked. He sounded as though he was about to burst into tears.

His dad's voice came from the doorway. "And we might have to consider sending Buddy back to Katie for more training."

NO! I went to hide beneath Noah's bed again, but he hid his face in my fur, crying. The sobs vibrated through my body.

"I won't let you!" his muffled voice said. There was a movement beside us and his mum kneeled, taking hold of Noah's shoulders to pull him to her.

"All right, we don't need to make any decisions just yet." She gave Noah's dad a warning glance over Noah's back as she rocked him gently in her arms.

I slunk beneath the bed again before Noah could stop me. "Buddy, come back here!" He called, reaching a hand to coax me out, but I scrambled back against the far wall. I didn't want anyone touching me and for the first time in my life, I didn't even want supper. I just wanted to be left alone. After all, if my

Humans didn't trust me ... how could *I* trust *them*?

"Come on, Noah. You need to eat." I listened to them all traipse out of the bedroom. "Let's leave the door open in case Buddy wants to join us." They padded down the stairs, one after the other.

Noah paused on a step, his eyes level with the landing. He looked back through the rails at me, still hiding beneath the bed. I wasn't sure if I imagined it, but I thought our eyes met. "I love you, Buddy." His voice floated over the air towards me but I didn't move. Then slowly, reluctantly, he followed his parents downstairs.

Later, I listened to Noah getting ready for bed; pulling on his pyjamas and cleaning his teeth, then the groan of the mattress as he got under his quilt, just above my head.

He snapped off the light and everything turned as dark and heavy as my heart felt right then.

"Buddy?" Noah's voice rang through the darkness. "Please come out." I heard him holding his breath as he waited.

Slowly, I inched out from beneath the bed. I leaped up on to his quilt and curled myself at his feet. He sat up and reached a hand out to tickle my ears.

We stayed there in silence for a few moments, and then he began to speak.

"Can you remember the day we brought you home from the Training Centre?" he asked.

Yes, you wore a baseball cap, I thought. *You threw it up in the air!* I remembered how bouncy and full of life he'd been that day. How had everything turned so sad?

"Your tail was wagging so hard in the dust, I knew you were excited to be mine." It was true. I remembered that *whoosh, whoosh,*

whoosh! I felt my throat constrict and I couldn't whine or yip or anything. I waited to see what he'd say next.

I heard him pull out something from behind his pillow and then the sound of pages turning. He snapped on his bedside lamp and showed me his photo album. "Look." I craned my head around and touched my nose to the corner of the page he'd opened it to. There was a new photo. It was a picture of me, the first day I'd joined Noah's family. Someone must have taken the photo when I wasn't looking.

I moved my chin to settle on his lap and for the first time since we'd got home, I looked him full in the face. His eyes brimmed with tears. "It'll be all right, Buddy. I promise you."

He snapped the light back off and we both settled down with a sigh. I crept up the bed so that we slept back to back, our spines touching. I lay there, letting his words sink into me. A sliver of moonlight pierced the curtains above the bed.

Oh, Noah, I thought. *How do I get anyone to understand the truth?*

Chapter Ten

Activity Day Is Go!

By the time I woke up the next morning, I really regretted skipping supper. I was starving! As soon as Noah got up and opened the bedroom door, I leaped off the bed and raced downstairs to where his dad was making breakfast. He quirked an eyebrow at me.

"So, you've stopped sulking, then?" He placed a bowl of food down in front of me and I wolfed it up in three mouthfuls. "Hungry?" he joked.

I ran out into the garden. Today was the

school Activity Day. The sun was high in the sky already and there was a gentle breeze. Despite everything that had happened yesterday, I couldn't help my spirits lifting just a little bit.

I heard Noah's voice from the kitchen and went to greet him – then froze in the doorway. He was wearing shorts, a T-shirt, trainers and a baseball cap, almost as though he...

"You look all dressed for Activity Day," his mum said carefully, placing a bowl of cereal in front of him.

"Mmmm," he said through a mouthful of muesli. His mum and dad shared an anxious glance over the top of his head. His mum sank into a seat beside him.

"You know we're only going to watch today, don't you? We talked about this last night." She placed a hand on his arm, but he shook her off.

"I know," he said. He didn't look at her.

"But I still want to wear my sports gear. Just in case."

"In case of what?" his dad said carefully. "You know you can't—"

Fortunately, the alarm went on someone's mobile phone. "Oops, come on! We're going to be late," said Noah's mum, taking a water bottle from the fridge and then looking at me hesitantly.

"We're not leaving him behind," Noah said darkly. He pushed past her with my lead and clipped it on. "Come on, Buddy. Let's go and have fun!"

"You won't be able to join in, Noah!" his mum called after him. He turned and stared at her. "I'm sorry. But I thought I'd made that clear." She threw me a look as though to say, *If Buddy can't be trusted to look after you...* Silence throbbed through the air, then Noah turned on his heel.

"Come on, Buddy," he said again, as he led

me out of the house and the two of us jumped into the car. Noah buried his face in my fur. At least *someone* loved me.

By the time we got to the sports arena, it looked as though the whole school had beaten us to it! Kids were chasing each other round the track and their parents had set out blankets on the benches, and were passing around bottles of water. Some of them had even made banners to cheer pupils on. And the noise! People were whistling and cheering, talking and calling. Activity Day was loud!

It was strange, though. As we moved through the crowd, no one made a fuss of me. By now, they were used to seeing me in the school with Noah, and kids loved to come over and slip me a morsel of food or stroke my fur. Some of them even tried to drag me to sit on their lap – have you ever tried having a Labrador on your lap? We're big dogs! But today – well, today, no one wanted to give me a treat. No one at all.

As we walked past a crowd of girls, they stared then quickly turned away, almost as though they'd been talking about us.

"Hello!" Noah called over, waving. One of them turned around and gave him a sad smile. Her glance fell to me and the smile faded.

I heard her whisper, "That's the dog that got Noah in trouble." I realized someone must have been spreading rumours about what had happened at the beach and it didn't take much to work out who.

Jake.

He hadn't just been lying to Lily's parents – now, he was telling fibs to the whole school.

I settled beneath a bench and gazed out from behind Noah's legs. His trainers kept kicking the ground impatiently, as though he wanted to be down there on the grass and I didn't blame him. Sprinklers were watering the lawn, sending rainbow arcs misting through the air and the scent of cut grass tickled my nostrils, along with the smell of hot dogs from a stand. I couldn't decide what I wanted more – a roll in the grass or a nice tasty hot dog! Anything to take my mind off what everyone was saying about me.

Down on the rounders pitch I spotted Lily immediately. She was wearing a white T-shirt, pink sneakers and had her hair in a long ponytail that poked out of the back of her baseball cap. She was practising with the bat and her arms looked strong in the sunshine. She was going to do brilliantly today, I could just tell.

I let out a bark of encouragement and Lily looked over at us. The moment she spotted us, her bat froze in mid-air. Then she let it fall to the ground and marched over, picking up her sister Amelia on the way.

Uh-oh, I thought. *What now? I didn't mean to bark at you, I'm sorry!*

"What's she doing?" Noah murmured. "The rounders match is due to start soon."

Lily came to stand before Noah, but instead of smiling and giving him a high five, her face looked serious.

"Noah, could I speak to you?" She jerked her head off towards a spare space on the bench. "In private, please?"

"Erm, all right." Noah glanced at his mum, who gave him a nod, and then he slid along the bench to talk to Lily. I started to go after them, but his mum held on to my lead.

I watched them talking, their heads so close they were almost touching. As they talked, Amelia took out her mobile phone and began to show Noah something. His frown melted away and he smiled and nodded eagerly. *What are they up to?*

The three of them came to stand before Noah's parents. "Can we show you something?" Lily asked.

"Er, sure..." his mum said, shrugging at his dad. Noah's sister, Lucy, stood a small distance apart, checking messages on her phone.

Lily started backing away. "Great. Just give us five minutes."

"All right, but if you're not back in five—"

Before she could finish her sentence, Lily caught up Noah and Amelia's hands and pulled them away across the arena. I let out a bark of exhilaration and raced after them.

What's going on? I wondered, as Lily let out a whoop of excitement. I guessed I'd just have to wait and see!

Chapter Eleven
The Game of Our Lives

As we raced across the field, the rounders teams emerged from one of the changing rooms, all in their kit and ready for the game. They each wore a white T-shirt, shorts and a coloured bib to show what team they were on. They were being led out by Jake, who looked thrilled to be at the head of the team wearing purple bibs. He waved to Lily and held out a bib to her, but she just ran even faster – straight past him!

Everyone's heads snapped round as they

watched us race past. "Where are you going?" Jake called after Lily. "The game's starting in ten minutes!"

But if Lily heard him, she didn't respond. Instead, she threw open the door to the arena office and marched over to a desk. As I followed them inside, panting hard, Noah shut the door behind us and the noise of the crowd outside fell away. A clock ticked loudly on the wall as we crowded round a wooden desk.

A woman was sitting behind the desk, a whistle on a cord hung round her neck. She was checking some numbers on a clipboard. I guessed she was in charge of the Activity Day – from her pursed lips, she looked like the type of person who was good at bossing people around. She wore a badge and I heard Noah whisper as he read the gold words etched in the plastic: *Mrs Kelly, Stadium Manager.*

"She must be new here," Lily whispered back to him. "We've never had a stadium manager before."

All her clothes were matching – she wore green trainers, a green tracksuit and a green baseball cap. She even had green eyes and green nail polish. This woman liked everything to be just so, I could tell. I wondered how she felt about slightly smelly Labradors.

"Excuse me, children aren't permitted in here," she said over the top of her clipboard. She hadn't even looked up. "And dogs should wait outside."

I gave a small howl and Noah shot me a warning glance to stay quiet. I slunk behind his legs and waited to hear what the woman would say next.

When no one moved, she finally glanced up. "I said OUT!"

But Lily was too busy fiddling with Amelia's phone to listen. She had pulled a cable out of her pocket and plugged it into the mobile, then handed it over to the woman. "Mrs Kelly, could you put these photos up on the big screen, please?" she asked, glancing out of the window towards the pitch.

Lily was brave, I had to give her that.

"I beg your pardon?" The woman's clipboard fell to the desk as she took the phone and cord from Lily and turned them over in her hand.

"In the camera folder," Lily explained. "It has photos in it that are very important for people to see." She swallowed hard. I sniffed the air and picked up on the scent – behind that brave face was a very nervous girl. "There's been a rumour flying around about Noah's Detection Dog—"

"And we want to put it right!" Noah interrupted.

What? This was the first I'd heard about that! I looked up at my friend. His face was bright red and I could see how agitated he was.

I touched the tip of my nose to the back of his hand. *Calm down, pal. I'm not that important.* But Noah's hands bunched into fists. *Wow!* I felt a sudden flush of pride. Noah cared as much as I did! Like me, he must have noticed how the kids at school had been turning their backs on me today.

For the first time, I allowed my heart to open to how that had really felt. I'd tried to be brave, but it had wounded me to the tip of my furry tail to see the children judging me to be something I wasn't. Katie had always said I had a heart of gold, but now people thought I was mean and unfaithful. I felt a flicker of hope – were Noah, Lily and Amelia about to put that right? I found myself panting with excitement.

Something shifted in Mrs Kelly's face. "A Detection Dog?" She leaned to one side so that she could get a better look at me as I hid behind Noah. She quirked her eyebrows.

"*This* dog?" There was a tone of disbelief in her voice and I tried hard not to feel offended. She came out from behind her desk and looked me up and down. "A Labrador, yes, I suppose that makes sense. They learn quickly." She spoke quietly, as though she was thinking out loud.

"Oh yes, they do!" Noah burst out, catching her words. "Buddy knows exactly what to do when I'm feeling faint. I'm anaemic, you see." I gave his hand a comforting lick.

Mrs Kelly hesitated, then pulled up the sleeve of her green tracksuit and showed us a bracelet. I recognized the small red symbol immediately – it was the sign for people who had epilepsy. I knew that inside the bracelet would be instructions in case she had a seizure and passed out. Just like Noah could pass out.

He gasped, his eyes lighting up. "You too?"

The woman smiled. "You never can tell, can you? I had a Detection Dog with me all through school and university." She folded her arms and leaned back against her desk. "Now, what's all this about rumours?"

Lily and Noah filled her in as quickly as they could. About the incident on the beach, and the story that Jake had told about how I'd run off and they'd had to follow me out to the caves. How Noah couldn't remember because he'd passed out.

"The rest is on here," Lily said, tapping her finger against the phone. "If you put the photos up on the screen, everyone will be able to see the truth for themselves, and then maybe…"

Mrs Kelly smiled. "Maybe people will believe in Buddy again." She came around the desk and chucked me under the chin. "As though they wouldn't believe in you!" She straightened up. "I know that these dogs get the best training ever. Buddy would never have been allowed to come home with you otherwise."

Noah slammed his hand into a fist and I jumped a little bit. "I knew it!"

Mrs Kelly went back to her desk and leaned down towards a microphone, pressing a red button on its base. There was a crackling sound and her voice echoed around the arena on loudspeakers. Noah, Amelia and Lily stared at each other, their eyes growing wide. This was really happening!

"Attention, everyone! Attention, please!" She gave us a wink before continuing. "There will be a short video display before the games commence."

Then she slipped the cable into the side of her laptop and began scrolling through. "Go outside and watch," she whispered to us. "I'll take it from here."

"Thank you!" Noah cried, before rushing over and spontaneously kissing Mrs Kelly on the cheek. Her face flushed pink right up to the tips of her ears! Amelia flung open the office door and we didn't waste any time – we had to see this along with everyone else!

The three of us ran to stand in front of the screen, and the rest of the school, including the parents, clustered round to watch behind us. Now we'd all see the truth. I could only hope that the truth was enough to keep Noah and me together and that I wouldn't need to go back for more training.

Jake arrived beside Lily. "What's happening?" he asked, tossing a ball from hand to hand.

"You'll see," Lily told him without taking her gaze from the screen.

We watched as the screen popped into life. At first, all we saw was the desktop of Mrs Kelly's laptop, but then the images Amelia had taken that day on the beach appeared. She had arrived to stand beside Lily and slipped her hand into her older sister's.

And as I watched, a story emerged, frozen

in time. A story I was all too familiar with. There was a picture of two boys striding out into the sea. A dog following – a very handsome dog! Hold on, it looked like… I gazed down at the glossy fur on my chest, then back up at the screen. It was me! *I* was following *them*. I hadn't abandoned Noah at all.

Of course, *I* already knew that – but here was proof, up in a giant version, for everyone else to see. I felt a shiver travel down my body as I glanced back over my shoulder at all the Humans watching. Their eyes were wide as they drank it all in. I turned back to the screen, just in time to see another photo of a boy collapsing between the waves – Noah!

My heartbeat began to speed up, as though it was happening all over again and I needed to remind myself that my friend was standing safely beside me. As we watched, his hand rested in my fur and I could feel his palm turn damp with sweat. It was difficult for him too, reliving the whole episode.

Then came a photo of frothy waves as a dog swam towards the boy, muzzle gaping for air, paws splashing through the water. It was me, swimming to rescue Noah! Then, finally, there was a photo of another boy standing uselessly on the rocks, watching. That was Jake.

"I was taking photos of the seagulls," Amelia explained now, "but then I noticed Jake and Noah wandering off towards the caves, and Buddy following them. I crept out of bed and showed Lily last night."

I remembered now that she'd been trying to tell us something back at the beach and no one would let her speak. Poor Amelia! But finally, we were all listening to her now.

Three figures pushed through the crowd of children, who were all clapping and cheering. "Let us through! He's our hero too!" It was Noah's mum and dad, along with his sister, Lucy.

They came to stand in front of me and his mum fell to her knees. She peppered my face with kisses and whispered the same word over and over again in my ear. "Sorry, sorry, sorry..."

I pulled back and gave her face a big, wet lick. Didn't she know Labradors were the most forgiving dogs in the world? *It's all right*, I tried to tell her. *You were only protecting Noah, same as me.*

Noah came to stand beside his sister. His mum reached up to kiss him, and his dad put an arm round his shoulders. They had a family hug and then Noah scooped up my lead and began to pull me away. "Let's get you home," he said, as he shouldered his way through the crowd.

"Hold on!" called a voice. We turned round – it was Lily.

What now? I thought. *I can't remember any other heroic moments I've had.* She wasn't going to show a photo of me eating my school dinner, was she? I didn't think that was very interesting – not unless I'd been given a second portion.

"Emily has glandular fever," she said breathlessly.

"Who's Emily?" Noah's dad asked, folding his arms.

Noah rolled his eyes. "She's a girl on our rounders team. She's the second best, after Lily."

"Third best!" Lily interrupted. "After Noah." She looked from his mum to his dad and back again. The look on her face said, *You know what I'm going to ask next.* Noah looked from face to face too, smiling hopefully.

Noah's dad began to shake his head. "No, Noah," he said. "You know what we agreed."

"No more sport? That's what *you* agreed,"

Noah said. "I never said yes." He smiled even wider. "Please?"

Lily stepped in front of him, holding her hands together in front of her chest. "PLEASE!"

A figure in green emerged from the crowd. Mrs Kelly. She was smiling broadly and tossing something in her cupped hand. It was a white shiny leather globe – a rounders ball. She threw it through the air towards Noah and he dropped my lead in order to catch it.

My heartbeat quickened and suddenly the crowd seemed to melt away. There was just me, a boy and a ball – the way it was always meant to be. I watched Noah's dad to see what he'd do next. After what felt like a million dog years, the frown melted from his face and I felt my tail begin to wag.

"Let Noah play," Lucy said. "Where's the harm?"

There was a moment of silence, then: "All

right," his dad said. Noah's mum had her arm linked through his and the two of them were grinning. "Just make sure Buddy stays close."

Lucy winked at us.

"Yes! Let's go and play rounders!" Noah cried, and we ran on to the pitch, with Lily jogging alongside. The game of our lives was on!

Chapter Twelve
A Surprise Gift

As we took our positions, a figure slunk away towards the changing room, pulling off his purple bib and dropping it on the ground – Jake.

"Let him go," Lily said. "We'll play without him." She grabbed his bib and handed it to Noah. After hesitating for a moment, he pulled it on, his hair all mussed up. He looked so cute!

"But we're still one person short," he said, pushing the hair out of his eyes.

Lily shrugged. "We'll just have to do our best." She strode over to the bowling position. Noah went to stand at one of the corners of the pitch, and bent low, resting his hands on his thighs, ready to catch the ball. He had a hard game ahead of him but I knew he could do it.

I paced the grass, just beyond the line of the pitch, being sure to stay close by. I raised my muzzle in the air and sniffed – all I could smell was adrenalin, sweat and the leather of the ball. Noah was good to go!

The ball swung through the air smoothly – a perfect throw from Lily! But the batter from the other team was good too, and he swung the wooden bat round confidently, sending the ball arcing through the air towards the far fence.

"Mine!" Noah cried, as he raced after the ball. I kept close to the side of the pitch, watching him carefully for any signs of faintness, but his face was flushed with energy. He leaped into the air but the ball flew over him, landing in the grass beside the fence. He didn't hesitate, racing to scoop it up, his face red from the exertion. Then he ran back and touched the ball against a post, just before the batter completed a full circuit. Out! The crowd roared and I spotted Noah's mum and dad on their feet.

Lily kept throwing and Noah and the others kept catching. They were doing really well, though being a person short meant that Noah hardly had a chance to stop running. I continued to keep a careful eye on him, but he seemed fine. In fact, he seemed more than fine – he seemed happy.

After a while, the other team had no batters left and it was time for the teams to swap sides. Several of Noah's teammates took their turn batting, but they were struggling to get round the pitch before being knocked out.

Finally, it was Noah's turn to try to hit the ball. He was the last one batting. I'll admit, I hadn't been able to completely keep up with the game, but from the tension I could smell in the air, I knew that if Noah didn't get round, the team would lose the game.

"Wish me luck, Buddy," he whispered, before taking a slug of water from a bottle. He placed the bottle down on a bench and took up the truncheon-shaped bat, swinging it through the air.

Mrs Kelly was watching from the side, the whistle pursed between her lips. She blew hard and announced, "Final innings!"

A girl in a yellow bib took a run up and launched the ball towards Noah. I found myself holding my breath as I watched. *One, two, three… Thwack!* Noah hit the ball hard and fast and it sliced through the air. It took all my self-control not to race after it!

He shot off immediately, being careful to run

outside the posts. The other team were spread across the field, shouting to each other. They'd lost sight of the ball! Noah was going to score a rounder! But as he raced towards the fourth post, I noticed him stagger slightly and slow down. Instantly, my nostrils flared as I caught a familiar scent and I noticed that Noah's face was pale too. He was going to faint!

I pushed past Mrs Kelly, not caring as she shouted after me. I had to get to Noah. He was still trying to run towards the next post and the rest of the team were too focused on the game to notice his body weaving across the grass. I ran up to him and touched my wet nose against his calf, which felt alive with heat. He was way too hot! *Stop running*, I urged him with every cell in my body. *You're going to faint!* He glanced down at me and attempted a brave smile.

"I'm all right," he tried to say, his breath coming out in short gasps. But then he started to slow his pace. I glanced over at his parents, who were watching hard from the side of the pitch. Noah's mum broke free from the crowd and began to stride across.

Noah slowed to a walk and rested his hands on his knees, bending over, his face suddenly cast in shadow. A droplet of sweat fell from his brow on to my nose. He reached out to pat my head as he took some deep, calming breaths. "Thanks, Buddy. You're right."

I'm always right, I wanted to tell him.

As his mum arrived by his side, he straightened up.

"Noah! Are you OK?" she asked anxiously.

He glanced over his shoulder. A boy was running back towards the pitch, a small white globe clutched in his hand. The other team had found the ball and any moment now, they'd be able to call Noah out.

His lips set in a firm line. "I am now. Just let me do this."

"Noah, I'm not sure—" his mum started to say but he was already jogging towards the fourth post. I ran alongside him – I wasn't going to let him out of my sight! As he reached out a hand to grasp it, the ball arced towards it. The ball bounced off the post, but it was too late. Noah had completed the circuit and got his rounder! More than that, he'd won the entire game for his team! Students flooded the field, calling out his name.

"Well done!" Lily cried, waving madly. She ran over to him and gave him a high five. "I know what you just did out there," she said quietly. "Now, go and rest!"

This time, Noah didn't argue. As he wandered over towards the bench, people crowded round. One girl even asked to take a selfie with him – Noah was a sporting superstar! Mrs Kelly watched from the back of the crowd, smiling broadly. She was holding something glittery in her hand.

"A team trophy!" Noah whispered, as he spotted it.

His dad patted his shoulder. "Well done. I'm proud of you." His glance fell on me. "And I'm sorry we didn't trust you, Buddy. We should have known better."

I wanted to tell him it was all right, but knew he wouldn't understand my barks, so I pushed my muzzle into his hand instead.

Suddenly, the crowd fell silent and I pulled my nose out to see what was happening. A figure had pushed his way through from the back of the crowd and now he was standing in front of Noah.

It was Jake. He must have been watching from the benches all this time. He was trembling! I found myself walking over to stand by his side. I don't like to see any Human upset, not even Humans who have lied to my best friend.

Noah glanced down at me and then up at

Jake's face. I could see what he was thinking. *If Buddy can forgive him, maybe I can too.* "What is it?" Noah asked.

Jake swallowed. "I wanted to say … I'm sorry." He kicked a toe through the dirt. "I just… I panicked. I didn't know what to do when you fainted in the sea and I felt useless. I knew it was my fault we were out there in the first place, but I couldn't…" His face turned red. "The truth was too hard to admit. So I blamed Buddy instead."

This time, I knew Jake was telling the truth and I leaned my flank against his leg to show Noah I trusted him.

Of course, Noah is clever and he noticed straight away.

"That's all right," he said. "We all panic sometimes." There was nothing in his voice – no anger, or resentment, no judgement – not even kindness. It was just a fact. Noah was right. We did all panic. I remembered how

I had panicked in the sea, not even sure if I could help Noah. It would only have taken one wrong decision for it all to turn into a disaster. That's all Jake had done – made one wrong decision.

"Come on, everyone!" Mrs Kelly called out. "It's the long jump next!" Kids cried out with delight and ran over to the oblong of sand, where a boy with long legs was warming up on the track and people were calling out encouragement.

Soon enough, we were alone. Even Noah's parents had drifted back to the bench, where they were packing up their picnic things.

Jake glanced over to where Lily was standing on a podium, holding Mrs Kelly's trophy above her head. She was laughing with delight as she passed the trophy around the rest of the team.

Jake sighed. "When you and Buddy arrived in school, Lily made a big fuss of you."

He scuffed a foot through the grass, not looking at either of us. "At first I was jealous. But then when you offered to pretend your gift to Lily was from both of us, I thought you and I could be friends. That's why I took you to the caves – well, that and the fact that I wanted to give Lily a present from myself." He shook his head and gave a shaky laugh. "Honestly, I don't know what I was thinking."

At the sound of his laugh, my heart melted. I mean – we Labradors are not known for holding a grudge. I padded across to Jake and dug my nose beneath his palm, urging him to stroke me. For once, he didn't pull away. It was strange. Now that I was up this close to Jake, I could smell his aromas and … they were good. A sweet combination of hope and energy and … was that chicken? A dog could always live in hope of a treat. I looked at his pockets but I couldn't see anything hidden there. Oh well.

Noah smiled shyly. "I'm sure we can all be friends," he said.

Jake raised his eyebrows. "We could play in the park next weekend?"

"Sure thing!" Noah was grinning broadly now. "Maybe get Amelia to take some action photos of us."

Jake's face coloured. "I promise I'll never do anything like that again – leading us into danger."

"Don't worry. Buddy here won't let you." I gave a small yip of agreement. I think I'd proved that no one hurt my owner! Noah was safe with me.

Jake glanced down at me. It was like he was seeing me properly for the first time and he ruffled my fur. The rest of the team gathered round, passing the trophy from person to person. Amelia appeared with her phone and started taking some more photos – she certainly liked snapping away with that thing!

Then someone came to kneel before me and lifted my paw to the trophy as though I was holding it.

Jake laughed. "First prize to Buddy – the Dog Who Dared!" I liked the sound of that.

Noah's mum and dad were waving from the gates. "Come on!" his dad called over. "Time to go home."

Noah fist-bumped with Jake and then we followed his parents out of the arena.

"Wait!" called a voice. "You forgot this!"

We turned round to see Lily running towards us, carrying the trophy. She shoved it into Noah's arms and it glinted in the sunshine, scattering light across Noah's freckles. He looked happier than I'd ever seen him. "Take care of it for the summer," Lily told him.

Noah grinned. "Thank you, Lily – for everything."

She shrugged. "Don't thank me. Just make

sure you get lots of practice in over the summer break!" Jake came to stand beside her and the two of them waved us off as we climbed into the car.

Today had been the best day ever! Noah placed the trophy on the back seat between us and we kept guard of it as we travelled home. Noah was a winner – but then he'd always been that in my eyes.

"What's for dinner?" Noah asked, catching his dad's eye in the rear-view mirror. "I'm starving!"

"Roast dinner," his dad told him. "I marinated the chicken last night."

My tummy gave a growl and I glanced inside the trophy, assessing. *Yup, I reckon you could fit a whole roast dinner in there.* Maybe if I was lucky, Noah would use it as a food bowl tonight! A dog could always hope.

Chapter Thirteen
Another Word for Friend

That evening I lay stretched out between Noah and his mum. She was perched on one end of the sofa and Noah was perched on the other. I have to admit, my body did take up most of the seating arrangement, especially after I'd wolfed down those tender morsels of chicken leg. The trophy sat sparkling on the windowsill – funnily enough, Noah hadn't let me eat my supper out of it.

His mum laughed now as she looked down at me. "I'm only letting you on here tonight," she told me. "It's a special treat to say thank you."

Earlier, Noah had phoned Katie at the Training Centre. I'd lain at his feet as he'd told her the whole story of how brave I'd been in the sea and how I'd taken care of him at the Activity Day. It was thrilling to hear how brilliant I'd been! No one even suggested I needed more training – in fact, Noah had repeated Katie's words from down the phone. That I needed a medal!

"We're calling him the Dog Who Dared!" Noah had finished, his toes tickling the fur under my chin. I wriggled with delight and rolled on to my back, holding my front paws up to beg him to stroke my tummy. As Noah ended the call he reached down and stroked his fingers across my soft belly. "Katie says hi," he told me and I gave a yip to say hi back.

Now that we'd had our supper, it was nearly time for bed. It had been a long couple of days

– a long couple of months! I couldn't believe how much had happened in the short time I'd been living with Noah and I could see it was a good job I'd come here. Who knows what would have happened if I hadn't been with him all those times he'd felt faint?

But soon, Noah's anaemia would be better and he might not need a Detection Dog any more. I gave a small whine of anxiety. What if they sent me back to Katie? Not for extra training, but for good. I mean, I liked Katie – but I *loved* Noah.

Noah must have picked up on my mood. As Lucy came to sit on the sofa next to her mum, he reached his arms around my neck. All four of us sat in a row, cuddling up next to each other. "We'll be together forever, won't we, Lucy?" I could feel the warmth of his breath in my fur.

Lucy gazed at the two of us. "I can't imagine life without Buddy," she said, reaching out for a snack from the coffee table. I lifted my muzzle hopefully, but she popped the biscuit into her mouth. Rude. "We'll never be without you or your tummy," she said, rubbing my fur.

Noah's dad's voice called through from the kitchen. "Time for bed, you guys."

"Yes, come on," their mum said.

Noah and Lucy rolled their eyes at each other. Reluctantly, the three of us climbed off the sofa and made our way upstairs. Noah picked up a sheaf of photos from a side table – Amelia had sent them over and Noah had printed them out before supper. Now, as he arranged them in his photo album, I hopped up on to the bed and looked over his elbow. There was Noah playing rounders, another one of him holding the trophy with Lily, and a final one of Noah with an arm draped across my shoulders. Who was I kidding? Noah was never going to get rid of me! I nudged my nose beneath his hand, forcing him to stroke my head. Then he kissed my nose. "It's you and me, Buddy," he said. "Best friends forever."

Noah got beneath the quilt, and I went to the bottom of the bed and turned in a circle three times before settling.

As Noah set the alarm on his mobile phone, a text message came through. "It's Lily," he said, reading it. "She says can I go cycling by the canal with her next weekend?"

"Aren't you meeting Jake in the park?" his dad asked, popping his head around the door.

"Maybe the three of us can go cycling *and* to the park," Noah said, wriggling down beneath his quilt. It was nice for him to have two good friends. *Three* good friends, if you counted me, which I did.

His dad snapped off the light and stood, silhouetted, in the doorway. He didn't say anything about Noah needing to be careful or that maybe he shouldn't do so much exercise.

I could feel the muscles relax in my haunches. "Night, Noah. Night, Buddy." Then he closed the door.

The two of us settled down. "Buddy?" Noah asked in the dark, after a short while. His voice was already sounding heavy with sleep. I nudged my nose into his hand. "I meant what I said. It's you and me forever, right?"

Always, I said inside my head. I gave his fingers a small lick to make sure he understood. I sensed him smile, then he turned over and soon his gentle snores vibrated down the bed.

I gazed up at the moon through a crack in the curtains. Was Jake looking at that moon too? And Lily? It felt as though a net of friendship was spread from home to home, keeping us all connected beneath that big white ball in the sky.

I curled myself up tighter as my eyelids grew heavy. Soon, I was dreaming too, my feet twitching in my sleep. I dreamed of chasing balls across a beach, running after Noah and leaping between Lily and Jake. Then the ball changed into a roast chicken and I found myself licking my lips as I gobbled it all up in my sleep. Yum, yum!

It doesn't take much to keep a dog happy. Just a boy, a ball and maybe a snack or two. Some might call me the Dog Who Dared, but I just call myself Buddy. Buddy is another word for friend, did you know that? And that's what I was – Noah's friend. That's all I'd ever wanted to be, even if it meant dragging him out of the sea. But soon, Noah would be able to do anything he wanted. He'd be the Boy Who Dared. Dared to take on the world – as long as he had a dog by his side.

Turn the page to discover a story of one dog's adventure to find his forever home...

ONE DOG'S ADVENTURE TO FIND HIS FOREVER HOME

Rolo's STORY

DOG'S EYE VIEW

BLAKE MORGAN

COMING SOON!

Chapter One
A Free Dog

Sniff sniff sniff. My nose twitched like crazy as it picked up the scent: warm and meaty and delicious. *Sniff sniff.* Dog food? *Sniff sniff.* A juicy bone? *Sniff sniff.* No, even better – steak!

My claws tapped on the kitchen floor as I closed in on my target, only to find that the food was high above me on the kitchen counter, where my paws couldn't reach.

That steak really does smell good, I thought to myself. *Although I'd prefer it served in a bowl on the floor. Perhaps with a side portion of bacon. But I'll take what I can get – I don't want to cut my tail off to spite my bottom.*

I scrambled on to a dining chair, rose up on my hind legs and clawed with my front paws at the kitchen counter. *I. Just. Can't. Reach.*

Aha – I know! I bounced up and down on the padded chair – *boing, boing, boing* – I was getting closer! After a few bounces, I was able to pull myself on to the counter. But just as I was about to sink my teeth in, the plate rocked off the edge and landed on the floor with a loud *clang!*

All of a sudden an angry voice shouted, "Mutt! Is that you, Mutt?" A tall, dark shape appeared from behind the kitchen door. It was one of those mean, furless creatures. A Two Leg. My owner.

A shiver of fear ran through me, right to the tip of my tail. My legs started to tremble and my heart was beating so loudly I could hear it in my ears. I leaped off the kitchen counter and turned to run – the steak now forgotten. My owner ran after me, chasing me out of the kitchen and into the garden.

"It's no use running away from me!" he shouted in his booming voice. "I'll catch you, you stupid dog!"

He was getting closer and closer, and when I turned to look and saw the rope he held in his hands, I almost tripped over my paws. My whole body trembled with fear. He was going to tie me up and leave me outside in the garden again. It was so cold and lonely out there – I couldn't bear the thought of it. Even a life as a stray would be better than that!

He was just reaching out to grab me when—

I woke up with a jolt. My legs were twitching frantically, as if I was still running. My dream had felt so real … because it *was* real. It had all happened, just like that, on the day I finally ran away. Apart from the steak – that really had been just a dream.

My nightmare brought it all back – how my owner would leave me on my own for days at a time, forget to feed me, shout at me when I'd done nothing wrong, tie me up outside during the cold winter nights. I might only be a mongrel mutt but no dog deserves to be treated that way. That's why I decided to stand on my own four paws – to make it by myself in the world – to run away and live *rrruff*. After all, how hard could it be?

That evening, almost a week since I'd left, I was outside, sheltering under a tree from the biting cold. "*Ow-ow-owww!*" The wind howled and I howled back, trying to scare it away. The moon looked like a pale grey ball just sitting there in the sky, as though waiting to be pounced on. It gave off a murky light that helped me to see in the darkness.

I was in a strange new place after travelling all day. *A patch of dry grass, some rusty old swings, railings all the way around ... must be a park*, I thought. Even though I was in unfamiliar territory, it was far too late to go any further, so I'd have to stay the night and get some sleep. As I lay down under a bench, my ears twitched at the sounds of unknown creatures rustling in the trees and bushes. I felt more alone than ever.

Grrrowl! That wasn't me – that was my stomach. I was so, so hungry. I hadn't eaten in ... I didn't know how long it had been, but it felt like many dog years. If only I knew my way around the park, then I could have hunted for some greasy food wrappers to lick. *Yum!*

As I thought about food, the hunger pains kept tugging at my insides and I let out a wail.

"*Ow-howl!*" But what was the use? Nobody was going to hear me and even if they did they wouldn't care. You just can't trust a Two Leg. At best they let you down and at worst they're as cruel as cats. I had to be my own master now. I had to keep going and never look back. I might have been suffering from the hunger and the cold, but it takes more than that to keep this doggo down!

I lifted my nose. A soft breeze had blown a strong smell of – *sniff* – trees, then something more promising – *sniff sniff* – maybe something good to eat – *sniff sniff* – something like – *sniff sniff* – FRUIT!

The smell reminded me of the only time I'd ever eaten fruit. I was trotting down the high street with my old owner on one of the few times he took me out for walkies. We got to a shop with fruit and vegetables on a stand outside. As we passed by, a plum rolled off on to the pavement and I gobbled it up before my owner could stop me – stone and all!

Now, I could smell the sticky-juicy-yumminess of plum once more. I followed the scent across the grass. It was as though I was on a lead – an invisible one that was pulling me towards the delicious fruit. I trotted along eagerly, my tail wagging with excitement.

There it was! A huge tree towered in front of me. There was a whole heap of plums scattered underneath. I gazed happily at the fruit. *You're mine, all mine!*

I scampered over to the tree, my tongue hanging out and dribble running down my furry chin. I'd almost reached the fruit when a frightening noise made me freeze.

"KRA! KRAAA!"

From high in the tree's branches, a flock of ravens flew out into the sky. They moved as one, like a pack of foxes, making my ears ache with their sharp screeching. *"KRA! KRAAA!"*

I can't speak a word of Raven, so I couldn't

understand a thing they were saying. But I did know this – they were heading straight for my fruit! The biggest one swooped down on the nearest plum and tore off a mouthful. I started to edge forwards slowly, carefully, to make my own claim, but the bird whipped its head round so I was level with its pointy beak. I was only a young pup, but I'd been around long enough to know that I shouldn't fight something with a beak sharper than my teeth!

When the biggest raven was full, the rest of the flock landed and started pecking the fruit to pieces. The large bird watched over them, making a *caw-caw-caw!* noise that sounded like it was laughing at me. Then all the other ravens finished eating and flew up into the sky. And all that was left behind was a pulpy mess of skin and stone.

So that was it then. No food for me. The only thing I could do was find somewhere to curl up and get some sleep. *Maybe I shouldn't have run away – at least I had food and shelter when I lived with my old owner*, I thought miserably. *Most days I'd get a few scraps to eat, like cold rice or pasta left over from his dinner. OK, so sometimes he'd completely forget to feed me but at least I didn't starve to death.*

No – I had to stop thinking like that. I couldn't just sit around feeling sorry for myself. I'd left home because I was unhappy there. If I just kept my tail up and carried on, I'd be much better off on my own. I trotted over to one of the benches – one with a pile of dried leaves underneath. I turned a circle three times to carve out a nest for myself, then flopped down heavily and rested my head on a paw.

I knew I'd feel better after a dog nap. Maybe tomorrow I'd find something even yummier than a plum. This thought cheered me up and got my tail wag-wag-wagging again.

Chapter Two
The Long Long Ears

The next morning, I stayed snoozing on the pile of leaves while the sun was high in the sky. When it hid behind the horizon again, I headed out. It was safer to move under the cover of darkness, when there was no chance of a Two Leg spotting me.

I walked down street after street. House, house, driveway, house, house, house, lawn. I *really* wanted to roll around in the grass and feel its velvety touch against my fur, but I knew it was too risky to get that close to where the Two Legs lived.

Every now and then I could smell a doggo inside one of the houses: the horrible, clean stench of a pet doggo that's just had a bath. *Yuck!* Ever since I went *rrruff*, I'd become a big fan of dirt. But as bad as the clean doggos smelled, each time I picked up their scent I couldn't help picturing them curled up on a squishy sofa, all safe and warm in front of a crackling fire. I imagined them being patted on their heads and thrown juicy bones from their owners' dinner plates. And for a moment, I wished I was one of those indoor doggos.

But then I caught sight of a dustbin next to a window where – *sniff* – I could smell – *sniff sniff* – bacon inside! Although it was raw and probably a bit old, bin bacon was heaps better than any Two Leg food.

Beside the bin, there was a length of short wall, so I rose up on my hind legs and hooked my front paws over the edge of it, hoisting myself up till I could clamber on to the bin with a *thunk!* I cringed at the sudden noise and jumped as the front door of the house creaked open and an unmistakable shape appeared. A Two Leg, alerted by the sound. I desperately wanted to dive into the bin and find the bacon I'd worked so hard for but there just wasn't time – the Two Leg would get to me before I got to the bacon. *Come on, now – quick! Run for it while you still can!*